For all those who have joined   Of Light.

RACINE

Book 2 of The Sisterhood Stories

ALISON CLARKE

ALISON CLARKE

ISBN-13: 978-1546988564

ISBN-10: 1546988564

ACKNOWLEDGMENTS

Thank you to all of you who continue to support me on this journey, and for those who have just entered the realm that is The Sisterhood.

RACINE

I woke up, gasping for air. I saw destruction; I saw terrified faces, and so much Fire. Everything was alight, but yet, surrounded by such darkness. Voices, with sonorous tones swimming in sorrow and regret, floated in the air. The time has now come. The time has now come. I was drowning in sweat. These nightmares were not unusual; they had become an almost nightly occurrence. What was I to do? What was my destiny? I felt the flow of the Ancestors. Soon, it would be time.

IT WOULD BE TIME.

I walked toward the fountain of Neptune and his nymphs and entered another world; one of mythology and magic, of mystery and mysticism of the ages. One that belonged to the Ancestors and their stories. Out of nowhere, a man dressed in rags appeared and pushed me hard. He glared at me before saying,

"You don't belong here." His eyes narrowed into slits. "You don't –"

The guard, stationed by the Supreme Court building, walked toward us causing the ragged man to take off. He asked if I was okay, but I wasn't – I really wasn't. I never am. I have never belonged, and when will that ever change? I shook my head, and walked away from him up the steps to the Library Of Congress, my mocha skin shining in the light.

The Library Of Congress consisted of three connected libraries: Thomas Jefferson, James Madison, and John Adams. The Jefferson Library, was the most decorative, and the oldest part of this magical space. For me, it symbolized peace and tranquility. It was particularly special because of the African-American scholar, Carter G. Woodson, who became known as the Father of Black History. He did his doctoral research at the Jefferson Library and found solace and inspiration there – the library was instrumental in the completion of his research. There was something almost magical about this library, named after the third President, Thomas Jefferson; the man who drafted *The Declaration of Independence*. The man who dared to dream in a new world: the pursuit of freedom. I admire him for that, but he wasn't perfect... I held my bag close, which contained a copy of Phillis Wheatley's poetry inside.

The Jefferson Library, the jewel of The Library Of Congress, had become like home to me. It was a place of peaceful meditation; an escape from all that was wrong with the world. I was currently researching Fabergé eggs, which held a strange fascination. There was no real reason, except for curiosity, but there was a likelihood I would be able to work it into my freelance work.

Since quitting my job as a teacher and taking up freelance copywriting for magazines, my life has changed a lot. Steve and I broke up. We had been high school sweethearts, then college, then engaged, all while I did a two year teaching certificate and was launched into a teaching world I had not been prepared for: chronic underfunding, students in such poverty they came to school with no winter jackets or boots. In the end, I couldn't do it anymore. Steve couldn't understand.

"Stick it out," he would say. "Get a permanent contract and a good pension."

I ignored him. I quit. Now, I was free and at The Library of Congress, recharging, resurfacing, trying to find some Solace. With my expired library card in my hand, I navigated the catacomb of passageways towards the office in one of the connecting libraries, the Madison Library. Punctuated by white lights, it was a maze I could only navigate by asking a whole bunch of people where this office was. After renewing my card, I returned to the Jefferson Library, leaving my belongings in the cloakroom before entering the Reading Room; the pearl of the Jefferson Library's oyster.

"You have a good day, ma'am," said an older black man, in uniform. "Enjoy yourself. It's one of the most beautiful libraries in the world."

I smiled. The world of knowledge awaited me.

It was as I was flipping through an art book on the Fabergé eggs; those mystical, magical orbs standing resplendent on ornate stands, that I heard a rustling noise. I stopped looking at the art book and scanned the room, questioning whether I had actually heard it or not.

"Racine, it is time. Racine, it is time. It is Time to follow."

I looked around but there was no one. Maybe I was dreaming? The nightmares had deprived me of proper sleep for nights now.

"Racine   Destiny   Racine   DESTINY   RACINE RACINE."

I looked around again but there was still nothing. The only conclusion was, I was crazy. My eyes took in the statues on the marble columns, which surrounded the Reading Room: one was a statue symbolizing Art, another Poetry. I waited for their eyes to move, for their lips to speak.

"Why?" I whispered. "What am I waiting for?"

The room remained silent.

I went back to work and tried to focus on the Fabergé Eggs. I had to write something; my rent was due in a month, and now living on my own, it was up to me to find my way. Things were going to be very lean for quite some time.

"Racine. Racine. It is TIME."

I shook the voices away but my eyes settled back onto the ten-foot figure with the gold letters that symbolized Art.

"Racine. Racine."

I felt myself lifted off the ground. Higher. Higher.

An angelic voice came to me in hushed tones, "You are a Druid. You are a Celt. You are a Griot. You are a Teller of Story. You are an Artisan of Words. You are the Messenger of Story. You are the Messenger of Narrative. You are the Wordsmith, the Griot, the Druid, the Celt, the West Indian. Racine, this is you, and the Chinese –"

I floated up and up. Up and up, faster and faster, toward the ceiling, toward the dome one-hundred-and-sixty-feet up. That never-ending circle of learning, the never ending odyssey that was life. Faster and faster, faster, and faster, I travelled like a jet of light. I closed my eyes against the impending crash; I was going to die. All at once, I felt an exhilarating rush of air against my body, like it was a foreshadowing of something that would change my life for the better.

I was being called to something beyond myself, like I was part of a bigger picture. Instinctively, I squeezed my eyes shut but the white light was so bright it shone through. When I did not crash, I opened my eyes to see seven circles of light surrounding me. I was in a library but the bookshelves floated in a circle, circling and circling, circling and circling, caught in their own orbit and I was their sun.

"What the hell!" I exclaimed. "What is happening? Am I dreaming?"

"Racine," said a soft voice. "It's all right."

Instantly, I felt at peace.

"You are safe. You are in good hands. You are loved. You are okay."

I looked up to see a beautiful woman with glowing tones of mahogany in her skin. She was wrapped in a fuchsia dress and diamonds sparkled in her jet black hair.

"You are loved. You are safe. Welcome to Origaen."

She was surrounded by six other women, all glowing in beautiful dresses of violet, champagne, tangerine, and amaranth.

I looked at her in disbelief. "Who are you? What's going on?"

"Racine, I'm sure you want to know why you are here."

I nodded.

The woman, surrounded by white, smiled and said, "Well, there are many reasons for you being here."

"Are you an angel?"

She smiled again. "No, I'm not an angel, not quite, but I'll tell you more of that in a moment. Now you need to know your history; it's time. I have to start from the beginning, from the times of yore – before you were born."

I was mesmerized. "What is my story?" I asked, desperate to know why my life was the way it was. Maybe I would get the answer for why I never fitted in, why my life was always going off track.

The woman in fuchsia robes nodded, as if she heard me, and I knew she did.

"You are in Origaen, a realm that relies on The Word; relies on Story. We are all artisans of the Papyrical; artisans of thought captured in vowels and consonants, black and white. We present the contradiction that provides clarity."

I nodded, despite being confused by her words.

"We are mystical beings, a guardian line that protects knowledge and learning through Story, and we have watched you from your time in the womb, to the time you were born, and beyond. This is your story, which means it is our story. I am sorry about what you have been through. I know you are hurting and you feel lost and alone."

She looked at me and tears fell down my cheeks.

"Racine, the time of not belonging, of feeling useless, is now over, and now you must embrace who you are. You must follow Destiny to forward your own story – your own narrative. You are part Druid, part Griot, part Angel, part Faerie. Long ago, with the start of our line at the genesis, an angel fell in love with a faerie, and their children became the guardians of The Word, the guardians of everything pure and healing. They were transcendent between Earth and the realm in between."

"What is my purpose?" I asked. "I feel something is missing but I don't know what. Tell me, what I'm supposed to do? I have this emptiness... but also this belief there is another reason for my existence."

The woman nodded again. She continued, "My name is Sevena, and I'm a Devenian. I am one of seven sisters who are part of this council. We watch over everything; we are guardians over all – love, acceptance, empathy, and knowledge. Our story is your story, and in telling it Racine, you will understand. We work with The One Above, and his many messengers, like The Seraphim. We are The Kindred: a fellowship of mystical women and men; some are animal, some in human form, like myself. The unicorns are my cousins, and so are selkies, and so are sirens, and so are giants. We all work in unison for this world – your universe and mine. There are others who help us; who help to work and live together in unison, parallel, across time. Our universe is parallel to yours, but it controls and regulates everything that happens on Earth."

"Am I a Devenian? Is this part of my story?"

Sevena smiled with a knowing look that flashed acknowledgement. She looked intently into my eyes.

"The Seraphim, who are Guardians of not only Time, but intelligence, creativity, compassion and love, as ordained by The One who had died for others so long ago. This is part of our destiny, and yours, but we are not Seraphim; we cross both angel and faerie worlds. Some say faeries were too passionate, too temperamental to be part of the upper realm, and so there came The Split. The proclamation made by The Chosen One decreed this, and so we came down to Earth, where we were ordained as Faeries of the Earth by Fergindaes, Father of all faeries, and his wife, his heart, Verdinia. Their son was Origanaes, and he fell in love with Orginia, an angel. With their union, their love created a race of beings who watch over the Human Ones, along with the Seraphim to guard truth and destiny. These are the Devenians: part angel and faerie. This is your Destiny, Racine, which was decided long before you were born. You are a Devenian. You are also part Celt and Part West Indian; you are a storyteller, a wordsmith. Your Asian blood –"

She stopped, seeing the look of confusion on my face. No one knew I was also of Chinese heritage. "How could you have known?" I asked, mystified by all she knew of me.

"I know all because of my Seraphim origins but also because of my faerie blood. There is a battle brewing, Racine; a battle of such great proportions that our two worlds will end. This is what we have to face, whether we like it or not." The woman in fuchsia shuddered. "The forces are gathering, the councils are preparing, talking to The Others, from different worlds to prepare for what is to pass."

"But what is to pass?" I asked quietly, concerned. I never thought life as I knew it might disappear in a heartbeat; a quick, faint heartbeat.

"There are many who don't want the gift knowledge, compassion, empathy, and love can bring; they want our worlds to be dominated by darkness, like in the beginning before there was Light. There are those who do not want unity, hope, and possibility. There are those who want hate, ignorance, cruelty, and greed to dominate and destroy everything good. We call them the Lynchantaens. They are demons not like the the Positvangaes, these demons just want to destroy." The woman in fuchsia trailed off and looked deep into my eyes.

"And where do I come in?" I asked, quietly.

"You are a warrior – as well as an artisan of words, Racine."

I suddenly see myself in a battle, suited up with silver armour and slicing heads off demonic creatures. I shivered. I had not seen such visions since I was a child. I looked back at Sevena.

"Yes, Racine, you are seeing your destiny. You have always known you were different from the others."

I nodded, smiling, but there were also tears in my eyes.

"Libraries have always been your sanctuary, your safe place," continued this magical Priestess of Light. "You have escaped to the Papyric realm when people harassed you, calling you ni –"

The woman shook the word away. Her sad eyes never left mine. "And so they harassed you, made fun of you, threw rocks at you because of the color of your skin. The library was always your safe place."

"I never had anywhere else to go," I whispered, still in tears from the cruel memories. "I only felt safe in a library. At home there was so much... and the world outside, well, you know," I shrug.

"I do know," replied the woman in fuchsia. "And I feel your pain, but you always felt better once you crossed the threshold of a library, didn't you?"

"Yes, I did," I said, remembering my horrible, hard childhood as a black child in an all-white neighborhood. "I always did."

"Well, we were watching over you and sending you positive thoughts, prayers, and an aura, an aura so powerful, that we healed you – healed your spirit, even if it was just temporary – and that's what we do for all who enter our world through the library. Whoever enters is always safe, always protected – and even when you leave, one of us is always watching over you, making sure you do not come to harm."

"I always felt safe when I left the library," I whispered quietly again. "I always did, and if the kids started running after me, and throwing rocks, I was always able to get away. They never caught up with me, and I always wondered…"

I looked up at Sevena and smiled.

"Racine, you would never come to any harm, because we have always watched over you, even though you didn't think anyone cared."

"But what about those who don't like to read, who don't appreciate Story?"

"They are also protected, Racine – but they do not have the gifts you do."

"And the battle, is it going to happen soon?"

"Sooner than you think, Racine, but before that happens I have to know one thing."

"What?" I asked quietly.

"You have to want to join this fight, to defeat the forces of darkness; you have to acknowledge you are a Devenian. The choice is yours."

I thought about what had happened earlier that day on the bus, how a teenage girl with light brown hair and blue eyes had refused to sit next to me, saying, "I won't sit next to a black person." No one had spoken up. No one had said a word. It was always up to me – that never changes. And so I told her off, and felt a bit better, but no one else did anything. Why didn't anyone stand up for me?

"I know things have been hard, Racine, I know –"

"But do you really? Have you been through what I've been through, and why would I want to save this world? So much has gone wrong."

"I thought of Ferguson, Charleston, South Carolina, Sandra Bland, and two years earlier, death... streetcar...Toronto - what happened to me on the bus... I thought about seeing children coming to school with their shoes falling apart, and their rumbling stomachs...Was that the world I wanted to save? And that's what I told Sevena.

"The choice will be yours," she answered.

"I am not the person you think I am. I think you have made a mistake."

"You will know what to do. It'll be up to you. The choice is yours."

I didn't want to be here anymore in this place of Light. Fear roils in my stomach, but just as my panic rose, I felt a wave of calm and my eyes started to close. My body moved across space and time and when I opened my eyes, I was sitting at the oak desk in The Library of Congress – part of the endless circle. A silver feather slowly fell as if answering my silent question, 'Was that real?'

A voice whispered, "The ending was the beginning, and the beginning was the –"

I walked out the doors, not knowing what to think. I

needed time – and I needed coffee. There was a coffee shop on Pennsylvania Avenue and Third Street. It was a beautiful coffee shop with a reading area on a separate level, close to Capitol Hill. It was as I was going down the stairs from the library, and about to pass Neptune's Court, that I stopped to look at the scene before me.

It was as if the sea nymphs were riding out of the water, about to gallop away on their sea horses ready for another adventure, while their king, Neptune, looked on. I closed my eyes, and imagined myself to be one of these beautiful but daring creatures, defying the orders of Poseidon, ready to venture off into different worlds – maybe to find love. I smiled.

The sound of crying pulled me from my daydream. A little girl sat on the steps near the fountain. She was so small, so tiny, in comparison to the building. She looked up and I could see in her eyes, she was lost. There had been a whole bunch of people at the front of the building, looking at the sculptural artwork but no one seemed to notice the little girl sobbing on the steps. They were all busy taking pictures. I took the little girl's hand. She was so tiny, with the brightest blue eyes, and short blonde hair. She took my hand without hesitation, and we walked to the coffee shop.

At the coffee shop, I talked with the staff. Eager to help,

a young woman in purple, with spiked hair and grey eyes, called the authorities. It wasn't long before a young couple appeared. They were visibly shaken.

The man approached our table and smiled.

"Thank you for taking care of our daughter. We thought she was with us, but when we looked around, she was gone. We have been looking all over. Thank you." Tears streamed down his face. "My wife," he looked at her. "She was beginning to imagine the worst, and –" He lowered his voice, "she is all we have."

I gently touched his hand. He looked straight into my eyes with his green eyes.

"We can never repay you." He smiled, feeling around his pocket. "But at least let us treat you to coffee – and here's my card should you ever need legal advice. I just got out of law school. I used to work here. It's funny how things work out. I know some of the staff here. Don't hesitate, okay? Thank you again, you are truly a force of light. We will never forget your kindness."

I nodded and smiled.

As I took the orange line into Oakton, my mind was made up. I knew what I had to do. As the bus weaved slowly away from the station, and Lady Lutania, the effervescent

Moon, came into my midst, it all started coming back: stories my grandmother told me about the nocturnal pearl in the sky, and the ceremonies that centered around Lady Lutania.

The next day, I walked into The Library of Congress, said, "Hi," to the cheery guy who worked in the cloak room, and saw the friendly librarian who wore a purple top that perfectly complimented her caramel complexion. I sat down at my favourite spot, with the Patroness of Art in the centre of my vision, and the Father of Time clock directly behind me. I knew exactly what to do. Once again, I floated up toward that glorious dome, proclaiming thought and knowledge from all corners of the earth, and seeing the woman, now in sumptuous cerulean robes greet me. Somehow, I knew I had come home.

"I knew you would come," she said, extending her arms wide.

THE FOREST

Dreams are Rivers. I heard the sound of a running brook. My grandmother always said, "Be Water..." but I never knew what she meant. Now would I? A woman walked effortlessly, her steps floating above the ground. She was a monarch. Her purple robes dazzled in the moonlight. Lady Lutania hovered overhead, a comforting Harbinger of Fortune.

"My name is Celestine, and I am Guardian of this forest: Queen of this Lair. Knowledge is my Currency. In the Past, people's souls were taken to make payment for crossing This Forest, and if people didn't make homage, through prayer or thought, their souls would be trapped in a jar made of elves' glass. But now, the Charter of The Forest did away with that, as there were abuses; people's souls were taken hostage –" Celestine looked back at me and continued. "And the Veraden, the council of the Wise Ones, banished the practice as a transgression against humanity. Now, all that is required is a thank you, a thought, a word, a feeling. It must be paid before you leave. You cannot leave without it; the Forest will not let you. The whisper of Zephyr's Daughter doesn't let you forget.

This is part of your history, your story, Herstory, if you will. It is time to be who you truly are. It is time to be your Destiny."

Three figures appeared before me; a knight with a red dragon as his symbol on his armour, a beautiful black woman surrounded by layers of colour, indigo, violet, orangey-red, black, and green, and another, an Asian woman, robed in White, with the Dragon also as her symbol. They flashed white, then red, then green, then an unforgettable blue, and then disappeared.

"Yes, they are coming for you," Celestine said. "To guide you and show you the way; to remind you what you have to do. Racine, you are the Key, the key to everything. Come with me now. You must learn. You must remember. You must know. The books are waiting to be read.

You will be going back in time, to learn your history from the beginning. Time is not on our side. Urania told me to make haste – so I will."

Celestine took my hand. "Close your eyes," she instructed.

When I did, my body felt like I was flying through space and time. I opened my eyes to discover I was once again in a library – none like I had ever seen. The books had wings, and were flapping all over the place. There was movement everywhere. The Library was like a Cathedral, airy, with a light I'd never seen before. The Library reminded me of Trinity College; the acres and acres of books, towering over you, a Harmony Papyrical... but all in Motion, floating across space and time.

Celestine snapped her fingers and a purple book, embossed with gold leaf, flew toward her. She took it and walked toward a circular oak desk. When I looked closer, I recognised one of the desks like in the Library of Congress. I gasped.

"Yes, Racine, the Library manifests what makes you feel most at home. And I know the Library has always been your shelter from the storm. You are safe here. You are Loved."

Tears came to my eyes.

"It's time to read and learn about your Ancestors, and those from Beyond. My eyebrow arched and Celestine responded, "You will know what I mean. Time is Fluid; the past, the present, and the future have converged. You are in the ebb and flow of Time, and Aventis will help you. She will be your guide."

A flash of Light appeared before me and a woman with cocoa skin and bright blue eyes greeted me. She gleamed red and white, and a large red rose appeared on her glossy black trident. She nodded and smiled. Celestine also smiled. She looked back at me.

"It is Time to be your Destiny. If you have any questions or need help, ask Aventis."

The Guardian in red and white nodded again. Celestine's green eyes flashed in mirth and something else I couldn't recognize, or understand. I then heard the words,

"Racine, be Water."

Celestine was communicating with me telepathically. I must have looked puzzled for she said, "You will understand in time." She looked over again at Aventis. "She is ready. It must BEGIN."

Aventis nodded and gently touched my head with her trident. I began to get sleepy, and pretty woozy; stars formed. I was moving, and someone was holding my hand. Was it Aventis?

When I opened my eyes, I was in a monastery made entirely out of oak trees. The tree trunks, stood tall and curved, which gave the building a serene, peaceful feeling that echoed through the ages. Men and women, draped in robes of red, white, or black, walked through the rooms, with hoods framing their faces.

I took a moment to take in everything, it was so extraordinary. Sat near the front of the room was a girl with unforgettable green eyes. She was with a man who looked like a teacher. He had a grave expression on his face.

"Someone had better come forward," he said quietly. "The Owl Guardian has told me The Impervicus Scroll is missing. It must be found."

A white owl appeared, shimmering like the moon. As she landed, she turned into a woman with pale skin. "Whoever has her, she must be returned," she said before disappearing in a flash. Aventis smiled before nodding and then disappearing, too. Before I knew it, I woke up, in a small room. It had bedding on the floor, like a mat.

I walked toward the mirror and peered into it, gasping at the sight of my green eyes, black hair, and ebony skin, which glimmered in the moonlight. I was just like the girl I had seen in the classroom. I ran my hand over the black robe I was wearing. Reflected in the distance was Lady Lutania. A knock on the door caused me to turn around. Despite my increasing anxiety, I answered it.

A girl stood at the door. "It's time for the evening rituals, the prayer to the Moon."

I had no idea what she was talking about.

"You should know by now," she said wrinkling her forehead. "It's part of your training, as a Druid. It is time to give homage to the Moon; Goddess of the Night, and to

Earth, Mother La Terre. They are both the reason for everything, and we must give our daily devotions. Why are you surprised? Come, it is time." The girl then said something in Latin, which I didn't know but I somehow understood. "Quaecumque Vera."

As we walked, she told me her name was Kiera and explained that as part of this order of Druids, the order that follows the moon, we also had to study martial arts.

"Patrick, leader of our order, strongly believes that every human being should have warrior training and know how to use a sword."

She led me into a room where exercises were taking place, legs and arms flying in the air akimbo. In another part of the room, an Asian man, wearing Chinese robes was barking orders, "Be like the animal. Flow, move, crouch, pounce, like a cat chasing a mouse, like a tiger hunting its prey. Memorize the movements, like the hopping of a bird, a magpie, crossing space and time. Be, Do, Be!"

A young man, with long blonde hair and blue eyes, crouched like a tiger and pounced on his invisible prey.

"Excellent," beamed the man in Chinese robes. "Excellent. Continue." The instructor looked at me. "Welcome," he said with a laugh. "Welcome to my class. Now, go, you are a Peacock."

I thought that strange, but did what I was told. I started to move like a peacock.

"Yes, yes, good."

I felt airier, lighter on my feet.

"Yes, yes. Now, do you see?"

I nodded.

I saw Kung fu, Tai chi, Jujitsu: the blocking, attacks on pressure points, strikes, joint locks – yes, everything connected. I was enjoying this class but soon it was time for me to be sent to the next one, scroll reading.

I was instructed just to sit and meditate with the scroll; touch the paper and think on it. Aventis appeared to me again and nodded.

"Now, child, you are beginning to see the great circle and the role of the Druids."

She disappeared.

My grandmother had told me of our Irish connection, from her West Indian roots, the island with the bearded trees. Dreams of rocks, black sea, and crashing shores. "Come, Come. It is time."

"Time for what," I whispered. "What am I supposed to do?"

"Learn, remember – Be."

A young girl in the robes of a novice, manifested and

asked, "Did you want to meet Lady Lutania, Goddess of The Moon?"

"Sure," I said, "I would love to."

Lady Lutania had eyes of blue fire, but they were kind. Her lips were a glimmering purple.

"You have come a long way," she said in low tones only I could hear. "You are learning well, Racine. You are learning about the Ancestors," she laughed. "And now you will know what to do. Take care, my child." She laughed again, her silver white hair, streaked with blue, flying in the wind. "You are –" She suddenly disappeared. "What happened to Lady Lutania?" asked the girl in the black robes.

"She had to go," I whispered. The girl looked confused. I spoke up. "She had to go." The novice Druid nodded. I was shocked. Lady Lutania knew. This journey across time and space. What I had seen, I couldn't believe. But that night, I had many dreams, and one kept coming back into my mind; it was a woman, a faerie with eyes of gold, and her hair a flaming burgundy, and her story, a journey under the sea, it permeated me, a Never Never land of sea and mist...

Two figures suddenly appeared before the sleeping Racine, who had now transformed into a green eyed druid.

A tall, young woman dressed in black robes, smiled, and said, "She is remembering; it is coming back. The call of the Ancestors, and their stories."

"Yes, Oppie." A large, but elegant dragon of purple, gold, green, and fuchsia nodded. "It is coming back. She will have to know all of this and more to be at the ready. Dear Sister, she must be, or –"

"Aurie, she will, don't be concerned." Oppie touched her shoulder. "It will be all right. Have faith. She will learn all that she needs to know. She is part of the circle, just like the one symbolized by that desk at The Library of Congress, in the Reading Room. Soon, she'll be ready. And I have hope, hope we can defeat this darkness. Hope we can overcome. That this world, and other worlds, different universes, will not perish. I must believe."

"And so will I, Sister," Aurie nodded. "So will I. For I don't even want to think about the alternative."

"We can't give up now; we have come so close, and the one she is dreaming of – Aquanaria... Do you remember?"

"Only the stories my mom told me as a child."

"Yes, for me, it is the same. And that is where Racine must Begin."

AQUANARIA

Misty Eyes. Aquanaria delved into the deep. She had escaped from Sangrian and now she had to find her way. As she travelled through the recesses of the deep, aquatic world, which was dotted with thatched roofed cottages, she became swan, then fish. She travelled deeper and deeper through the recesses of The Deep and finally, she came upon a water spirit known as a Miengua, who had long dark locks, and piercing almond eyes. An aura of yellow, red, and orange surrounded him in a nautical rainbow. Aquanaria asked him where she was and he replied, "Longonia."

The name was vaguely familiar, she had heard it from somewhere, but she didn't feel any the wiser on what she should be doing.

"Go to the Sea goddess, Nefertiti, daughter of Poseidon," the sea sprite said seeing her confusion.

Aquanaria nodded and swam around the corner, where there was a palace of shimmering pearls. She went inside, having felt a real sense of urgency. Something was wrong. She heard a voice.

"It's missing. It's missing! The Scepter –" Starfish,

dolphins, and an octopus, who were all wearing sentinel uniforms, greeted her. She raised her eyebrows.

"This way," they all said together.

Before she knew it, she was walking into a classically ornamented room, with ceilings that shone with the colors of the rainbow, and where Corinthian columns reminiscent of Greek temples, held up the vast roof. Statues of all sorts decorated the room, including one of Nefertiti's father, Poseidon. The little known daughter of this noble aquatic family presided on her throne made of seaweed, anemones, coral, and stardust. As daughter to a god, she was one of the Mystics.

Aquanaria's grandmother had told her stories of such beings.

"Welcome, Aquanaria, welcome. We were expecting you," said Nefertiti with a smile.

"Why am I here?" I asked.

"You are here because you fled from Sangrian. Now, you have shelter. You are safe. But for your safety, there is a price."

"But I just accidentally found your world," I pleaded.

"Are there ever such things as accidents?" Nefertiti asked.

"Well, I –"

"No, you don't know, you are too young."

Aquanaria thought differently, and Nefertiti smiled in response.

"Aquanaria, they will take you to be outfitted with weapons and –"

"I didn't sign up for this –" she protested.

"Go, you must pay back your debt. GO!"

These people were strange, stranger even than the faerie folk, but it seemed she had no choice. She was all alone and there was no way she could fight her way out. Nefertiti nodded in return, then left.

Two women dressed in purple seaweed, escorted her to a fitting room where they dressed her hurriedly in armour and chainmail before presenting her with a sword and dagger. The finishing touch was a shield, which she was assured would save her life. From here, Aquanaria could hear the battle already raging. She was full of fear. She had no idea what she was meant to do – she hadn't been trained for such a life. Stumbling out of the castle, she saw nereids and krakens, against selkies, stargines (shape-shifters who would change from starfish to human form). Poseidon was in the background, spitting out orders as the enemy pelted them with the poison of jellyfish, and spears tainted with arsenic and mercury.

Bodies drifted to the bottom of the ocean floor. Aquanaria shivered, knowing she might not make it. Blow by blow. Kick. Punch. Somehow, even though she was in water, she had no problem doing any of her martial arts. The energy flowed through her. Eventually, the enemy gave up; they were no match for Poseidon's formidable force.

The war was won, but many souls had been lost. Aquanaria looked round and seeing a man who had been stabbed in the neck, she swam over to help him. He was bleeding profusely but she was able to use her Faerie powers to heal him. The young man opened his eyes of unforgettable greenish-purple and smiled, in thanks. Maybe, there was a reason for her to be here. Nefertiti smiled at Aquanaria and the young man: a connection had been made. It had just begun. A spark that would ricochet through the ages.

Angelaes, from the realm Wyrniverdon, a force of angels and faeries committed to fighting for all of humanity – mortal and faerie, also smiled, in unison. She had looked into a mirror, framed with gold, and saw Aquanaria, the young man, and Nefertiti. It had just begun.

RACINE AND THE ORDER
OF THE MOON

A new day had started; I had gotten up, and was now eating a herbal salad dressed in olive oil. I then got dressed, put on some purple robes, and went to another class – this one was on meditations on life, the universe – how we're all connected. A young man, dressed in blue robes, started answering the question to, "How are we all connected?"

He gave such an eloquent reply that I forgot I was in the room. His name was Willen, and from that point on, he was always in my thoughts...

As the student responded to the Master, head down, wrapped in his student robes of blue, the colour of water, the colour of creativity, he started to chant.

"To be human, to be of man, or woman, is to love, to respect, to cherish. To respect Nature is to be one with her – listen to her rhythms, like the goddess, Gaia; to take no more than is necessary.

"To hunt, to clothe oneself, all from animal origins – from the animal skins. To meditate deep in Nature, to listen to the wind of the trees. To touch the great oak, and listen to her stories, to understand her origins. For she is the Tree of Life, from where it all began.

"Lightning awakens her, Lightning is sparked by her. Life energy flows within and through her, for we are all associated with Mother Oak: and we only are at the tip of learning her mysteries. As the Earth, Mother Gaia, only reveals what we need to know.

"This, Master, is what I know from your teachings. The answers are always right in front of us, but we have to pay attention. Socrates knew this: we have to be still and listen. We have to listen to that guiding force, or as he said, the daemona. The life force, guiding angel, whatever it is for you, we must listen; and let it take us on a journey, which is our Destiny. Humility is also key, and listening to others. For using your voice, expressing yourself, is important, but just as important is listening to the voices of others."

"And so ego, concern for oneself, is that important?" the Master asked.

"Only insofar as you must always protect yourself, retain dignity and self-respect. But more important, is to have concern for others, and as much as possible, lift others up. The defensive arts are only necessary if one is threatened, as in the example of our Buddhist brothers."

The Master nodded. Willen opened his eyes. As if the

whole class sensed this, they also opened their eyes and slowly got up.

"It is now time for deep meditation," said the Master, whose name was Clorik. "Meditation and the class for self-defense, as taught by our Buddhist brother, Xendu."

Everyone nodded, including me, and we all went to the Room of Light. Cushions were everywhere; colourful and unique, with silk threads running throughout, spinning tales of stars, unicorns, Greek gods and goddesses. Images of oak trees, the rowan, and runes also punctuated the silk landscape. There was even one of Socrates, the one guided by a benign spirit, or his daemona. It was all possible in this cloistered monastery of image and sound.

I was attending another class, one about the healing properties of the oak. I listened carefully. Then mistletoe, the healing properties it had, the bark of the oak; it was fascinating. Mother Nature had so many gifts to help humanity.

Why would humankind not treat her with kindness? Instead our world was destroying her for greed and profit. As I mulled over this, I saw a shape in the distance; an image, swirling in the mist. I got closer, peering into the silver curtain of air. It looked like a sword. Excalibur; Gleaming. It stayed for a moment, as if wanting my attention, then it disappeared, leaving in the air's wake, a rowan tree, with red berries gleaming, and frost dripping off it. The color of the berries reflected in the water, as if it was dripping blood. Something was wrong. I thought of what to do and started running. The wind through the trees was a warning, singing with short screams.

I kept running until I saw a clearing then jumped over the drystone wall and saw a red cloak flying in the wind. I got closer. Silver armour, breastplate, helmet. It was a Roman soldier. I looked to the left and there was a young peasant girl, attending to her cow, giving it some water. She was probably taking it to the marketplace in the small town nearby. The look of fear etched in her face reminded me of granite carvings. A sword was hovering closer to her throat.

"Halt!" I shouted. "What are you doing? She means you no harm. Unhand her, now!"

The soldier looked at me, with a dark smile. "And who is this? Are you a slave?"

"No, I am a free woman, now unhand her."

The soldier threw his head back in laughter. He then looked at me, narrowing his eyes: "You will pay for that remark. Prepare to die, slave girl, Prepare to –"

I closed my eyes and a sword appeared in my hand. It

gleamed in the sunlight. Madame Soleil showered it with a golden glow. I got into position.

"You will unhand her," I commanded.

The Roman soldier grinned, slyly. His sword edged closer to the peasant girl's throat, drawing a bit of blood. I flew into action, my body flowing like the air around me, becoming a fury of Karate, Jujitsu, and Tai chi. I jumped onto a nearby tree, sprang off it and knocked the soldier's sword out of his hand with such force, he was thrown off his horse.

I moved quickly, as if all the gods and goddesses were in my blood, weaving back and forth, like a dance.

The soldier started to get up and was fighting with me, but I quickly kicked him in the groin, and he doubled over. I kicked him again and he fell to the ground. Quickly, I put my sword to his throat.

"You will leave now. Go. You are not wanted here."

He nodded, got on his horse, and galloped away.

"Thank you, mistress," gasped the young girl, who was about fourteen. "Thank you. I don't know what I would have done. I just don't know –"

"You're all right. It's going to be okay. Are you hurt?"

The girl shook her head. "I was only giving my cow water, before I was going to market to sell her. My family needs coin, right away. I was doing my duty when the Roman came upon my path. If you hadn't come along –"

"Don't think about that now. You are safe."

"You, you are a Druid, the one from the order who follow the moon. You are the ones who practice the form of self-defense, which originated in the East, and came here through the Buddhist brothers. You are from that order?"

"You have heard of us?"

"Yes, I wanted to join but my parents would not permit it. But, I have heard of women warriors, Celtic... and the Vikings..."

I smiled, remembering the story of Boadicea; a story which hasn't unfolded yet, but the ramifications will reverberate throughout time.

"The Celtic women are known for their bravery, and you have their strength, their presence. Are you from a Celtic tribe? The Gauls perhaps...?"

"I have Celtic blood," I replied. "It is a long story. I have a lot of different ancestral lines in my blood."

"I can see that. I also know many people with your likeness, who navigate different worlds, through different blood lines. I would like to join your order. I would like to become a warrior, as well as a philosophical thinker, which I know is the main philosophy of the Druids. But my mother told me your order is different, as they believe in more physical self-defense, which is what I agree with. I think it is important to be able to defend ourselves against the malicious; those with evil intent. Would I be able to join you?"

"I can take you to one of the Masters. He can decide what can be done."

The young girl looked at the cow.

"Don't be concerned about that. Someone will take it to market for you. Your family will get coin."

The young girl nodded, and went with me. I talked to one of the elders of the order. He had dark brown eyes, with flaming red hair, and a beard to follow suit. He looked intently at the girl.

"Yes, she will do. She has the fire. The Spark. She is willing to learn."

For some orders, learning the Druid ways took twenty years, but in this order, it depended more on the students' abilities. Sometimes, the Druid would give the blessing to join in ten years instead of twenty. The girl didn't care how long it took.

"I am ready. If it takes me twenty years, or more, I am committed. I will do your bidding, and learn your ways. I need a purpose, and being a village girl, marrying a farmer, is not my destiny. I know there is something more out there, and your line, dedicated to Lady Lutania, shows this is true. I would be honoured to join your order."

The Master nodded. "You are ready." He looked at me. "Thank you. And for what you did, saving her. This will never be forgotten, for this order believes in advocating for people; for those who need justice. I know my ideas are in conflict with many of the other Druid orders, but I think it is important. For us to survive, we must be able to arm ourselves and fight."

I nodded. "I agree. I thank you for what you are teaching me. I will never forget."

"I know you won't, and you have many gifts; they will serve you well. Continue to study and learn. You will go far, as it has been foretold." He nodded.

I walked away with the girl to the main compound, a fortress made sturdy with the trunks of oak and rowan.

"Yes, that one, she will go far. I have seen. There is a darkness coming, and she will be the only one who can eradicate it. She will lead the others through the darkness. But without her..." He shivered. "All of humanity will be lost. I will continue to pray to the moon, Lady Lutania, as well as Mother Gaia, for guidance. Listening to the wind, the rustling of the trees, listening to the music of the Earth for the answer. The darkness is coming, and she must be at the ready."

It was now night, and the silver harbinger blinked. Lady Lutania agreed, as if she already knew. And the sister goddess of the moon, Phoebe, suspended in air, only seen by a few, nodded her head; her familiar, Lady Lutania, a short span away. The Sisterhood would be needed. The Army of Light must be trained. For the forces of darkness were soon coming to sweep across the land, and yes, this was just The Beginning.

LESSONS

The next class was led by a Gaul, who was known for the ways of the sword. You looked into his face and you knew he enjoyed training these novice Druids. And, despite my short time here, I was getting more proficient. Also, with my martial arts training, as well as imitating the movements of the animals found in nature, my gait and movements were getting stronger and stronger every day. This caught the attention of the blonde, young man from earlier, the one with startling blue eyes. I was a force. He sensed it. He also sensed my determination. Somehow, he knew I was not from this place, not just physically, but from a different time. I knew he wouldn't tell anyone but would keep these musings to himself. At the end of class, he walked up to me. We continued walking up a grassy knoll, overlooking the mountains, and there, in the cliff of rock opposite, was a lone rowan tree, striving to make it her home, despite all the odds.

"Naeva."

I nodded for that's what I called myself.

"You move like one of the gods. You move with the dexterity and coordination of a cat. You pounce like a tiger.

How do you do it?" he asked.

"I don't know," I said. "I just go with the flow."

He laughed. "That is not a saying I have ever heard. You are not from this world, are you Naeva? You are from a different time."

I was silent.

"Your secret is safe with me."

I paused for a moment. "You must not tell anyone."

He nodded. We talked about Herodotus, and how he paid tribute to the Egyptians, writing how they were a profound influence on Greek culture. We talked about the priestess of Dodona, the Egyptian one, and the influence she had on the world. We talked about Socrates, and his daemona: the possibility of a celestial being guiding his thoughts and actions.

"Do you believe in such a thing, Naeva?"

"Well," I said, "anything is possible."

The young man, Willen, nodded his head in agreement. Our talks and walks went on for hours when we were not in classes. The Masters all smiled, especially the lead elder. He said to himself, "Those two would soon be ready." He smiled.

One night, looking at Lady Lutania, Willen's lips brushed against mine. I was surprised at this, but when he did it, my body seemed to separate and I felt different. I was now on the outside, looking in. I saw a tall, willowy young woman, with green eyes, dark mahogany skin, and long jet black hair, wearing a blue cloak. Aventis had then appeared and was standing, shining in her red and white robes; the red rose from her trident seemed to be aflame. She nodded.

"It was time," I thought.

And so the story ended, but it also continued, as I saw the couple, Willen and Naeva finish their last bit of training. They had decided to marry. They went to the Master. He nodded.

"Your training in this world, with this order, has ended, and another one has begun. Go forth, for you, your children, are part of a chain, and the manifestations will ring through time."

"The darkness is coming, isn't it Master?" asked Naeva.

"Yes, it is; in waves. A Celtic order of monks will be saving that knowledge in books. And after that, there will be waves of darkness and Light, but there is something else coming that will threaten to end all humanity. You, and your children, are the key."

Naeva and Willen both nodded.

"We will be ready," they said together.

"I know," responded the Master. "Go forth, my children. I, and all of us here, have taught you all we know. Now, it is time for another journey. Go forth."

They nodded and left.

I understood. My heart was beating fast in my chest. Naeva was one of my Ancestors, part of my blood line. She was the Druid my grandmother had told me about. I remember her stories about the willowy woman with many gifts, including prophecy. Aventis looked into my eyes and uttered one word, "Yes."

The winds picked up and she started to howl and shriek. The trees bent with the wind, waving in the aerial ocean. Aventis put out her hand and I took it. We were enveloped in a golden ball of light, moving through the air, above this unforgettable Druid order. We jettisoned to the stars, to the Milky Way, and beyond – going another course, another destination, for it was about Story, it was about origin, and I was ready, to learn more about my story, Herstory.

Aventis took me back to the library, the library of the flying books and bookcases.

"So," said Celestine, smiling, "you have learned a part of your story; the Druids and the Willowy One."

I nodded, still in disbelief.

"Well, here is another part of your ancestry. Another part of Story, which starts on one side of the world, goes to another, and then, takes an interesting turn. Seek, Racine." Celestine again smiled.

A purple book, embossed with gold letters stood out, shining at me, as if speaking my name. I was meant to open it. I flipped open the book, lovingly touching the cover. I looked at the one word in purple – Cuchalaen. And then, a shape of a ring with an image of two intertwining hearts emerged. I looked further down the page and the words seemed to move, almost like snakes. I touched the letters, and they stood still for a moment before getting bigger, and bigger. My eyes started to get sleepy and then I felt the touch of Aventis; saw the torrents of waves, a fishing village, and the words,

"It now begins."

CUCHALEAN

I wanted adventure, and securing employment as a blacksmith in the West Indies was the only way. I had damaged a fishing boat and had to pay the captain back; but I didn't mind. Wanting out of this fishing village, something called to me, something from the Seven Seas. I got my contract and six months later, I was on a ship.

It was made out of oak, and the front of the ship was in the shape of a woman. Half fish, half woman – a mermaid. She was all adorned in blue and purple, and her hair was a ravenous black. Previously, I had stood and looked at her from the dock. I knew mysteries and magic awaited. I remembered the fairy tales I was told as a child, like Jack and the Beanstalk, and knew even then, there was more out there; it was not just the stuff of fiction. I remembered the tales of my uncle, going out on the sea and encountering huge whales, even sharks, on their expeditions. Yes, I was on my way to better employment; the West Indies, part of a realm not known to me. I knew my life would never be the same.

As the ship set sail, I was excited. I was going to leave this provincial life and go somewhere new. It was time. I had always felt like I didn't belong.

"Would there ever be a place where I did?" I sighed.

It was a feeling I wanted to erase. As I fell asleep, Lady Lutania hovered overhead. The night was a comforting blanket, decorated with golden orbs of Light. It was calm. I was dreaming of angels and faeries, dragons, too, and then,

"Ahoy, pirates! The ship is under siege! Men, get to your weapons!"

As I was just a passenger, who did some chores to pay for his fare, I didn't have any weapons. Instead, I just hid. A voice bellowed from the darkness,

"The dowry, for the ones from Barbati frondoso – it's here! Get it, men! Protect it!"

A man appeared with a brightly coloured head scarf and striped pantaloons. The other men were similarly dressed, and some also wore one earring, which emitted a mysteriously bright gold. Many spoke in a language I didn't understand. Things were tossed about, maps of previous adventures overturned, until a blanket was pushed aside and a strange sight was beholden. A bright blue treasure chest, inlaid with mother of pearl. It shone a bright blue.

One of the pirates, speaking another language, took a step right toward it and touched the lid.

"No, Hichem," said the pirate with skin the same colour

as mine. "Don't touch – "

But Hichem did, and the chest opened, nearly blinding all the men below deck. The light from the chest touched Hichem and suddenly, he disappeared. Only dust of a fine blue appeared.

"Damnation!" swore the pirate with the bright blue eyes and pale skin. "This treasure is not worth human lives –" He was about to turn around when a blue ray shot out from the treasure chest, killing him instantly. Then, one of the other lead pirates, who wore pantaloons of a bright purple, quickly ran toward the second dead man, who had also just turned into dust. He stood back in disbelief. This pirate, tall, towering, with mocha skin, told the other men to stand back. A child came out of nowhere, probably the son of the man with blue eyes. The pirate tried to stop him, but the child, distressed, kept running, saying,

"Papa!"

The bright light of blue was heading for the child when I jumped into action and grabbed the little boy, stopping him from getting too close to the second pile of dust. By doing so, unfortunately, the blue ray of light hit me and I fell unconscious.

Voices were swimming around in my head.

"What are we going to do with this bloke? The fella

just came out of nowhere. We just wanted the treasure, not this!"

I then heard the words of the towering lead pirate. It was like music. I didn't understand the meaning of his words, but somehow, I felt comforted. Then, I felt my body moving. I seemed to have been put on another ship. Then, it docked, and I was being moved again. I had regained consciousness, but couldn't open my eyes. It was like my eyes were being weighed down by a force not of this world. I felt movement again, like I was put on some kind of moving animal, and was travelling somewhere.

It seemed like days, but what would I know, for I was in a deep, dark sleep. I saw visions of corpses with rotting flesh, and miles of tombstones. Strange dreams, indeed.

When I finally woke, I felt something in the air; it was hot and dry, and the sun was a bright red ball of fire. The vegetation was different. The animals were different. There were creatures with one hump on their backs, and huts made of what looked like straw. This was a lot different from my fishing village; the only world I had ever known. I blinked, then opened my eyes again. No, nothing had changed. It wasn't a dream.

A young woman, with beautiful mocha skin approached me, with a bowl of white grains, and some kind of meat, and vegetables. I tasted it. It was good, and I gestured to her that I liked the taste. She nodded then walked away after bowing her head. I smiled back. She wore a blue dress of many layers; different types of beautiful cloth. Indigo, purple, red, black – they radiated a beautiful sheen. She wore a headdress matching several of the colours in her dress. She glowed.

After a couple of weeks, I got up and took in my surroundings. The air was hot, but there was also lush vegetation. It appeared in patches on the land. I breathed in the air; it was fresh. I must be in the mountains. How far up, I didn't know. My chest felt a lot better, much better than it had in years. I was often used to having chesty coughs, and coughing up yellow phlegm. My mother always told me to get rid of it – don't keep that shite down. She was right. But here, my chest was clear, and my breathing unimpaired.

I walked around. The beautiful girl with the colourful dress was nowhere to be seen. I kept walking and came across a blacksmith's forge. Inside, was the lead pirate, hammering away at something. There was a row of beautiful rings, some silver, some gold; some had emeralds, some had rubies, others were bedecked with diamonds. I gasped. I had never seen such beauty – such finery. The pirate smiled, his green eyes sparkling, and his mahogany skin shimmering in the sunlight. Before you know it, I said,

"I would like to learn how."

When the pirate misunderstood me, for good reason, I gestured to him, and his work. The man then smiled.

Over the next year, the pirate, whose name was Anis, showed me all the skills in making the beautiful rings. I was happy to be learning these skills; I could take them back to my fishing village and charge a fortune. I would be rich! As if the pirate knew what I was thinking, he uttered one word,

"Stay."

I had been teaching him some English, and the pirate had taught me some of his language. But it was his daughter, Cylia, who picked up the most English. She showed she was quite gifted with languages. One day, as we both sat on a hill, looking at Lady Lutania overhead, Cylia said, "What is it like, this Ireland?"

I said, "It's beautiful, but also very sad. We have had so many invaders, and the latest one wants to strip us of our language and culture. The one of Orange, King William, only wants our children to be taught in schools that ban our Catholic religion and Irish culture."

Cylia nodded. "Yes, that is sad indeed. You, what

would you like to accomplish?"

"I want to set up a blacksmith's shop, and sell rings, like the ones your father makes, and make a good living. I think I could make a lot of coin. I don't think I'm meant to be a fisherman."

I then explained how I almost sank a neighbour's fishing boat and Cylia laughed.

"No, it's not for you, your Destiny is elsewhere."

"Yes," I said, "it is." I looked deeply into her caramel eyes. "Yes, it's elsewhere."

Cylia smiled. I took her hand. I knew she was part of my Story. I had found my home.

I told the blacksmith I wanted to take Cylia back with me to Ireland. The blacksmith became irate.

"No," he said, in English. "Danger."

He had heard stories of his people being taken in chains, and never heard of again. He would not allow that to happen to his daughter. Cylia was sad. She wanted to go with me; not only did she love me, she trusted me. I had told her those horrors in the Americas did not happen in Ireland. I was the Irishman from across the seas, and she wanted to spend her life with me. I would take care of her. Love her. Cherish her. Love knew no boundaries. Love was love. She talked to her father, but he walked off in a rage;

she never broached the topic again.

It was soon time, and I would have to leave. I had learned all I could. Now, it was time to go back. I wanted to start anew, create something, and have others be a part of it. I loved my time here, but the greenery of Ireland, the people, and the unforgettable waters, still stirred my heart. But, my true love, my only love, could not come.

As I made ready for the journey down the mountain and to the ocean, I kissed Cylia good-bye with a peck on her cheek, which I knew symbolized more. Later, making sure we were alone, I kissed her on the lips.

"I love you, my heart," I whispered.

She nodded. I was about to leave, when I saw a silhouette, looming large over me. It was the Master Blacksmith, Anis. His one earring shone like a golden orb.

"Protect," he said, softly but firmly.

He held my hand in his own. He then took my hand, and placed it over his daughter's. I nodded. I would always take care of her, my Cylia. Anis knew. He smiled. Cylia went with me, her Irishman, in a ship commandeered by Anis' fellow pirates. We would be safe. Cylia, dressed in a dark cloak, stood by my side.

When we reached Ireland, we walked to my cottage; the one I lived in with my mother. She was happy to see me, and when I introduced her to Cylia, I was not surprised that she took her into her arms, and her heart. Cylia, from beyond the ocean, was now a part of us, all of us. Celebrations ensued. We were later married. It was not unusual for this village to welcome people of a mahogany sheen. There were others who had Cylia's likeness, and through talking to many of them, discovered they understood her language. My wife was a harmonizing spark to the community, and she often told stories of her homeland to many people, of different backgrounds, but were connected through the Power of Story. Possibility. A type of magic. And so, another Story had begun.

SCHOOL OF THE MOON

No more sorrows of the dust... souls turning to rust...

I was walking to school, in the light of Lady Lutania. It was night, a time of calm rivers of peace and solitude. Others would have thought it unusual. King William of Orange had put out a decree for the Irish, saying if they were to attend school, they would not be taught their culture, their language, their history. It would be driven out. It wasn't important.

My mother came from across the ocean. She was beautiful, with glowing mahogany skin. There were another people of the same sheen, who lived in the mountains not far away, and they came down to the village sometimes to sell their wares; a cloth, like silk, but which had a beautiful glow, as well as texture, as if touched by magic. It was said they were touched by the sea – that their spirit came from another world. There were those who said they came from the lands of desert, sycamore trees, and monuments exuding mythology, like The Sphinx.

My mother conversed with them in her language; the language of the desert – of a region of a continent far from here. But love was the equalizer, and in her husband, my father, Cuchalaen, my mother found a home.

My father made jewelry, beautiful jewelry, which people came to buy from all around. They bought it for cherished ones, for loved ones. For those pieces of gold and silver were made with love, I knew that. That love was Light.

This village accepted my mother as part of the family, the love between a dark-haired Irishman and a beautiful woman from across the seas. For love was magic, and within that love, acceptance, which binds all.

I symbolized that love. Me, Amira, and now, I walked to the hedge school, for I loved to learn. One day, I would like to be a teacher, but was that possible in these times? For the Irish were not allowed to teach. Not now...

And so, I walked down the path to an abandoned barn where there was a light in the window. I approached the faded red barn, going past the drystone wall, where there were children of various ages and grade levels.

I loved to learn. Books were portals, and through the magic of Story, I could travel anywhere. I could be part of Jason's Odyssey. I could learn about Socrates and Herodotus. The languages of Latin, Irish, and Greek. I could learn, and the vessel was the Power of Story.

As I listened to the teacher reciting a poem, I closed my

eyes and listened. Then, I looked up. The moon, Lady Lutania, hung above. I closed my eyes again to the rhythm of the teacher's words and began to dream. And so the celestial connection was made, through time and space, space and time; entering the cosmos and travelling many millennia into the future of the orchestra of stars, the nebula, and the sheer wonder of the Milky Way.

BOREALIS

Looking into the heart of a dark star drove her mad. Borealis shivered. This is what she had read in one of her History books; about a Star goddess, who specialized in celestial prophecy, who depended too much on dark magic to increase her powers. Borealis would never go in that direction. The price was too high. She didn't want that to be her fate, but as she sat on an asteroid in the cosmos, listening to the sounds of a newborn star, it was on her mind.

Her assignment, as part of her Celestial goddess training, was to listen and interpret the sounds of a newborn star; decipher what the Mother of the Stars, Selenia, was saying – what message she had for the cosmos.

Borealis listened intently, but to no avail. She did not know what the star was saying. She looked at her notes and looked again. She closed her eyes in prayer, and listened to the star's heartbeat. She was sitting in a yoga position. Nothing. She tried again, sensed a shooting star, and opened her eyes. Borealis watched it pass by: it was probably on the way to Earth. She needed to pass the time. She was getting frustrated. Borealis closed her eyes again.

Still nothing.

There was a strange silence in the atmosphere, even though the cosmos was filled with harmonic hums, and moans. She thought about her school, and the drama going on in it. One girl had plagiarized another student's paper about a village; in a world called Wyrniverdon. A place where there was an alliance between the faeries and angels. All of them had different gifts. This student would have gotten away with it, but the instructor had a sense something wasn't right. The instructor had just touched the sheets of stardust, and knew something was wrong. She went to the archives and looked it up. There was a paper not only about the same topic, but the same argument, word for word. Nothing was changed in this girl's paper. Nothing. Bournairis was kicked out of Star goddesses' school. Good riddance!

Askinance was another one; she was having an affair with her instructor, and was getting good grades. This was a college, and the girls were not kids, but was that really appropriate? Borealis surely didn't think so.

"Beau, what's up?" It was Kindaes from the neighbouring all-boys' academy.

"Not much, I'm just trying to get the coordinates from this star to get a reading. I'm trying to listen to her heartbeat and her pulse, to see what she is feeling, what she is thinking, and how the message of Selenia is reverberating through her. All stars are prophetic; they carry the messages of Selenia. I'm just trying to understand but it's just not coming through."

"Ummmm... we have to do something similar in our academy, and it's been a tough go. Maybe, if you look at her light levels – the brightness of her shine. Dark glasses, which filtered out the star's light, suddenly appeared on Borealis' face. To look too closely at a star could blind someone – even a future Star goddess. With her old fashioned lenses, which ironically made her look like a grandma, she peered deeper into the star.

"Yes, I see what you mean." She wrote more notes on her star gilded paper. "I do. Thanks, bud. I was really stuck."

"Anytime," said Kindaes, smiling, and then winked. "Give me a shout if you need any more help."

"Will do," said Borealis, smiling. "Will do."

Borealis kept taking notes. She then closed her eyes, still sitting in a yoga position. She listened. Then she was alarmed. She got up and flew to the portal, which led to the academy. "The instructor, Venus, needed to know about this," she thought.

And when Borealis told her, the instructor's eyes opened up in shock. The world, the universe, the galaxies, the cosmos, would never be the same, and it was something that involved a planet with four oceans and six continents. Borealis shivered. She had never seen the instructor look so terrified.

A SPARK

A star was born, full of light, fire, and colour: violets, pinks, electric orange, a buffet of colour. The Milky Way was humming, the meteorites left a musical footprint, and a Star goddess-in-waiting was kneeling upon a neighbouring star.

Illumini was struggling at the Star Goddess Academy. She didn't know how to read the stars, she didn't know how to give comfort or guidance to a dying star, she didn't know how to ride the Milky Way to survey all the goings-on in the different galaxies; she didn't even know how to read a map of the cosmos to find any black holes, which was very important to ensure there were no suspicious entities sneaking through. Black holes were a gateway to other worlds.

There were angels and faeries who had knowledge of these things, who worked with the celestial realm. The sisters from the realm Wyrniverdon were highly knowledgeable in these matters, but it was slow going for Illumini. Even with their guidance, she was still having difficulty. She didn't think she was going to pass this program. She didn't think she was going to finish.

A woman appeared with a trident, and it was unique, as it had a symbol of a rose. She smiled at Illumini, then disappeared.

"What was that about?" She thought to herself. *"I must be studying too much. I need a break."* She flew to another cosmos, right through a nebula. It opened up, and she entered the cafeteria of her academy. There was chatting, buzzing, and the murmuring of different voices. Illumini saw Borealis, but thought she should leave her alone, as she looked like she was deep in thought. What was on Borealis' mind? *"I hope it's not too serious,"* Illumini thought. *"Maybe I'll just give her some space."* She decided to join another table of girls.

"I'm going to the next level, the Master class, when this is all over. I can't wait to be a part of it, and the professor who teaches it is so Hot!"

Illumini snorted. "Is that all you think about, Beaumaris; is that all that's on your mind?"

The rest of the table laughed nervously.

"Well, at least I have something to think about, and something to look forward to. You've been moping all week! What's wrong with you?"

There was silence at the table.

"I've got a lot on my mind, and the semester has been

really busy."

"So you can't cut it, eh?" laughed Beaumaris.

"I'm doin' just fine."

"That's not what Professor Oclearis said. Someone's not doing well in all of her classes."

The silence continued.

"I don't know what you heard, so you can just…"

"Girls," said a woman with purple hair, and green eyes, "what's going on? Can't we just behave decently, and set an example for the younger ones?"

The silence continued. No one wanted to be in this conversation, well, except for …

"Everything is under control, Miss Peale. It's all good," quipped Beaumaris.

"Apparently not, if people are shouting."

"Well, you just came across a heated debate."

"Not so much if it's about a student's grades, which is a confidential matter between instructor and student. The vacuum of sound continued. Everyone knew Beaumaris' aunt was an instructor at the school, and known for telling everyone's secrets, especially those of other instructors. "I expected better from you, Beaumaris."

The whole cafeteria became silent.

"Well, I'm sure Beaumaris will now be the wiser, and

didn't know the harm she was causing," Illumini said ever so sweetly. "I'm sure she won't make that mistake from now on."

"Well, Illumini, I hope so. For the universe can't rely on gossipers and naysayers. We'll all have to stand together when the time comes."

"We'll be ready," Illumini said.

"I know you'll be," said Miss Peale, quietly. "And remember, believe in yourself, for that conquers all." She looked at me with a gleam in her green eyes. Then, she walked away.

"What did that mean?" chirped Nuwella.

"Oh, shut up!" snarled Beaumaris. "What's it to you anyhow?"

Nuwella shrugged her shoulders and went back to eating her lunch of starberries and cosmic salad, flavoured with stardust. Illumini suddenly felt at ease. There were people who actually cared; people who wanted her to do well. Maybe she would finish this program after all.

JOURNEY

Illumini was observing a star, an older star, which had been around for many millennia. Her heartbeat had echoed throughout the ages, and made a sonorous echo with all the other stars and celestial beings in the universe. For every star had a song. Illumini was trying to hear the music of this star when she heard screams. She quickly flew to the source, and saw a student from the all-boys' academy almost being sucked into a black hole. He didn't have on his gravity belt, which would have prevented him from being sucked in. He was desperately holding on to an older star, which was also going to be sucked into this dark realm.

"Hold on," shouted Illumini. "Help is on the way!"

She closed her eyes and a lasso of stardust wrapped around the boy and his star. She pulled, with her mind, the both of them until they were safe – millions of miles away from the portal of Death. "Thanks, Illumini," gushed the young student, who went by the name of Kilaen. "I could have been toast – literally!"

"Anytime, Kilaen. Anytime!" Illumini beamed. It felt good to help someone. It felt good someone appreciated her and her gifts.

"Well done, Illumini," laughed Miss Peale. "I knew you could do it." She winked. "Sometimes, we surprise ourselves."

Miss Peale was surrounded by a pink, violet, and a champagne aura. Today, she looked like a British nanny, and Illumini thought of Mary Poppins.

"I look forward to seeing you on graduation day," Miss Peale said, nodding her head.

Illumini smiled. She would make it. She then looked over at Borealis. She would go over and talk to her. The girl, dressed in purple stardust, gave a small smile.

"Yes," Illumini thought, "she needs some company. Maybe then, I can find out what's going on. She is one of the few girls who make me feel at home, like I belong. I want to make sure she's okay."

As Illumini got closer to the table, Borealis' smile got wider. Illumini smiled back. She knew she had made the right decision. It was also one of the pledges of the academy to help one in need; especially a fellow sister.

***

I woke up, and the teacher, Peter, was looking down at me

with a smile. The teacher thought, *"This student, Amira, had a faraway expression in her green eyes, a feeling that was quite not of this world."*

But Peter of the School of the Moon, didn't mind. Amira always participated in class, and she recited poetry beautifully; she loved Yeats – especially that poem about calling a child to join the realm of Faerie. Sometimes, he wondered, *"Was Amira a faerie herself?"* He sensed something different – a mystical sensibility other students didn't have. He knew her mother, who came across the seas, from the mountains not far from a civilization that the Greeks admired and paid homage to. There was something there, but he couldn't quite put his finger on it. Something... But then thought, *"What do I know?"*

He was a dreamer himself, and maybe he was reading too much into things... But, as he put his books away, he waved goodbye to Amira. If only all children like her had a passion, a delight for learning, the world would be a better place. The Man of Orange was trying to destroy a culture. Well, it wouldn't happen. It wouldn't do! The Irish spirit was too strong – and no, the people would not allow it. The breadth, depth, of not only Irish language and culture, but the propensity to learn more, was so prevalent, students often stepped into the linguistic realm of Greek, Latin, and so on. The hunger for knowledge would not be quelled by this oppressive monarchy. The Irish people were too strong for that, and would not accept anything else. Education was the key, and he knew that; it was the key to everything, and without it, they had nothing.

****

The class was now over. I got up and Peter, the teacher, was waving good-bye. I waved back, as I walked away. I was always dreaming, whether I was asleep or awake, and sometimes, I felt like I didn't belong in this world – that I should be somewhere else, maybe a different time. Earlier, the teacher in the abandoned barn was talking about a unique historian. Under the glowing realm of Lady Lutania, the teacher talked about Herodotus, who spun story with history. Many Greeks called him a spinner of fairy tales, but I knew some of what he had seen and written about would manifest, maybe not in my lifetime, but would become concrete. Civilizations he mentioned in his books would later be dug up, and his words proven to be true.

I also thought of the Egyptians, ahead of their time, in science, culture, and how the Greeks, like Herodotus, paid tribute and acknowledged their influence on the Greek culture. Would this be appreciated or seen in future generations? I didn't know, but my mother also told me about the great Ancient Egyptians, and their extensive civilization, which had loomed not far from my mother's homeland. My mother told me, later that night as we walked home with my brother. Once in my bed, I went into a deep sleep, clutching a book my teacher had lent me about Herodotus, and his travels.

Through Story, I would travel, once more.

THE CEDARS

They moaned, and creaked. Creaked and moaned. The Light, which came down from the heavens, sparked with flame and energy; electrons charged the forest below. It was these that created the sentient beings of The Illuminatus, who walked the Earth, and guarded the Forest of Cedar trees. Their bark transformed into vessels for the Ancient Egyptian empire, and became a magical element in their papyrical scrolls.

These Creatures of Light, Illuminatus mainly walked at night.

One beautiful creature, Syterie, was walking through this hinterland, under the watchful guise of Lady Lutania, when she came upon a lost stranger.

"Are you far from home?" she whispered, looking into his dark eyes and at his jet black hair.

He nodded.

"I will guide your way. Follow."

The young man was about to tell her where his village was, but she put up a hand. "I already know. Come."

She walked with him, her aura flashing on and off as she walked. She was a crescendo of orange, yellow, red, and a subtle silhouette of blue.

Aban had never seen anything like it. The villagers talked about mystical beings, which walked the Earth. They were Guardians of The Forest, but he didn't believe it. But now, he shook his head – anything was possible. They walked through mountains, hills, and valleys.

Finally, Aban was home. He had left to see other family in a nearby village, but had taken a wrong turn somewhere. He had followed the wrong path and ended up in the Forests of The Cedar.

He looked at Syterie. "I can't thank you enough."

She nodded. "Keep safe," she said quietly.

Aban thought that was the last he would see of Syterie, but he was wrong. He was reading some faerie folklore, on papyric scrolls, when he thought of Syterie. He was also reading about Herodotus, and Socrates. He thought about the daemona, that mystical spirit Socrates claimed to be guiding him. He thought deeply about this, wondering, *"Could it be? Was it possible?"*

After seeing Syterie, he came to the conclusion that anything was possible. As he was thinking this, Syterie flashed in front of him. He gasped.

"You are here. From where?"

"I heard you wanted to have conversation; to talk about

the things you were thinking. Well, here it is. Here I am. Let us talk about Herodotus, and the people known as the Egyptians, forerunners of thought and culture. Let us begin." She hesitated, and then continued, "But first, there is a story that must be told. It is of Alecia, one of the priestesses of the oracle, Dodona."

Aban nodded. How lucky he was to have met this woman – this Celestial Being of Light.

ALECIA

The stars were the navigators: this was the language of the Ancient Egyptians. The gods and goddesses charted time, and worked with Cronos, and his daughter Aventis. The Cosmos was alight with light and sound. Alecia was enamoured. She loved the sound the stars made: that song sung so sweetly. Those golden orbs with their aura.

Alecia was the chosen one, out of seven sisters, to be a priestess at Thebes. But she knew there was a longer journey involved. She knew there was more out there than what her parents thought. Her mother had a feeling and supported her in what she wanted to do but her father, no. Why not marry a good husband? He would be a good addition to the family and bring with him a dowry of the finest cattle; beef to last, especially through the cooler months, and when there were times of drought. But Alecia did not want that kind of life. She wanted magic and adventure.

Alecia had a dream that night.

Two black Pigeons, chattering in a language no one could understand.

The Only Ones.

She saw herself on a ship with a horse head. The sun burns in the sky. It is a beam of fire casting a silhouette. New shores lapped by the deep aquatic blue of the sea; a backdrop to the white temples, their columns wrapped with white fecundity, wreaths.

She sees.

She

Suddenly

SEES.

Alecia woke up, thinking of what was to come. When Lady Lutania was a full shining silver orb, she left what she knew as home, for another. She went by camel to this temple in Thebes – an oblong building made of stone. She learnt the ways of prophecy, meditation – and she just listened. Some people came to the temple just to be heard by the gods. That's all people ever wanted – to be heard.

One night, some men came. They were dressed in tunics, which covered their chests and shoulders. They wore conical hats ending in a top knot. Their voices were different, their accents reminding her of stormy seas. Forcibly, they took her by camel, and then by boat to another place; to a pristine lair of blue, aquatic blue. She listened and learned, learned and listened; the different accents, the different rhythms. And then she came upon a temple with white columns, high roofs, and sculptures all around it dedicated to the gods – like Zeus, who was this father of Olympus. A god very much like one of the gods she worshipped from home. But now, this was her new home and she knew she would never see Thebes again. Alecia looked. Was this for her?

In her mind, there was the flash of a juniper tree, with its dark brown trunk, twisting. Its green leaves shooting out, and the purple berries, which left a dark stain on the skin.

She thought of how her grandmother saw the tree as an entranceway to a different world. Her grandmother was prophetic, a soothsayer; her vision hurtling through time and space, echoing throughout millennia.

In this new place, called Dodona, one of the pinnacles of Ancient Greek civilization, Alecia was faced with a grove of oak trees, which were a manifestation of Zeus, but also a symbol of learning and wisdom. She went behind the temple and closed her eyes; the heartbeat of the stars, was in her mind's eye. The jet black sky and the stars, unforgettable discs of Light. She continued to listen to the meditative and soothing stars.

She continued to close her eyes, and then suddenly, she was absorbed into the oak grove. Her sisters, the other priestesses, were frantically searching for her, but to no avail. Alecia was gone. The priestesses did not know what to do. They consulted with the senior oracle. All she said was, "She'll find her way. She will find her way home, back to us."

Despite the senior oracle's reassurances, the priestesses decided to go on a quest to bring Alecia back to safety. Even though it was only three months, these women were already attached to Alecia and they were all very close. All priestesses genuinely cared about each other. It was time to bring their sister home.

A TALE OF FOUR WOMEN

The first stop was The Castle of the Moon, the Manor of Phoebian. The Moon goddess, Phoebe, sister goddess to Lady Lutania, dressed in purple, green, and white, greeted the three women. She was hauntingly beautiful.

"We are here to find Alecia; the priestess from Dodona?"

Phoebe nodded. "She is not here."

Something shiny appeared in her hand.

"A comb," she said quietly. "You will know what to do."

The women gasped, as it was made out of the skin of the moon, and shone with stars. They asked to stay the night. The goddess agreed.

After they left the castle, they closed their eyes, and flew to another part of the cosmos; to the home of a celestial library. Books appeared, suspended in air. Birds of purple, green and gold twittered and tweeted. The chirp of the birds created another aura, making it hard to enter the library, so they used the comb to separate it and create an opening.

Once done, they flew inside. Many tomes, hung from

the air inside. Stars streaked across the expanse. Bookcases also hung in the air, and some flew around having wings, just like in Celestine's library that was part of the Magical Forest.

A doorway opened up in one of the flying books and the women flew through. Then, the ground had found their feet. They kept walking. Hums, whirrs and beeps were in the foreground. It was all pitch black, except for flowing pages of papyrus, and another form of manuscript, which the priestesses did not see before. They were mysteriously unfamiliar, but they knew it was because they came from a different time. This library, this tribute to the literary, was a gateway to another dimension.

The three priestesses flew up to another part of the library, which was formed in the shape of a pyramid. The three women all gasped at what they had seen; what they had known, and now? Another gateway opened, and inside were Beings of Light: Light and Sound.

Their gowns had hieroglyphic symbols on them, which moved as the women moved. On their gowns were also bits of the cedar, found in that forest of old; which had given birth to ships, and whose resin was used to embalm the dead. The women continued to move.

"We are looking for Alecia, our sister of Dodona," the

women cried.

Immediately, images of golden leaves appeared on trees, which also emanated silver. Two of them burst into flame.

One of the bodies of Light also found in the Great Forest of Cedar, spoke, "She is not here. She is in another realm, another world. Someone requires her audience. She is being asked to..."

"To what?" asked the women together. "What?"

The Illuminatus would not answer. There was just silence.

JUNIPER

Purple berries, dripping their juice. The love of the ages, healing, transportational, going into different worlds. The Gateway to – ? The three priestesses continued on their journey, flying through the universe, their dresses flirting with nebula, solar systems, cobwebs of stardust. They passed through galaxies; the Milky Way, Andromeda, until they got to a large, gnarled tree, bursting with green leaves, and purple fruit. They got closer. Suddenly, The Illuminatus appeared. They gave the three women an emerald necklace. The three women got even closer. A small circle of light glowed in the middle of the trunk. Verandaes, one of the priestesses, took the necklace, and touched it to the trunk and it opened up a doorway.

The three sisters of magic night and prophecy sailed in, their dresses flowing behind them in the wind. They walked around. A lion of stone hovered over them. They walked toward it and saw something in the distance. As they got closer, they saw their sister, Alecia, enclosed in a glass cage. Alecia knocked furiously on the wall of it.

"Get me out of here, Sisters. There is a Darkness

coming, and we must all flee!"

The three priestesses got closer.

Thebian said, "She's trapped. What can we do? There is no other implement that was given to us."

Zerian thought for a moment. There was a song in her head. A song, Phoebe, sister goddess of the Moon, had sung to them. The song went like this:

Borealis, Orchealis. Where is it?
Place to call your own, place to be home.
Place where the ibis caws and moans,
Moans and caws, not in sadness,
But in joy, for even when times are hard,
A struggle, there will be ones around you,
To see yourself, not a mask, not a ghost,
 But your true self, shining though...
A love, the most powerful love of all,
The love you have for yourself,
The best friend you will ever have,
 The one you see in the mirror,
The one that carries you on this earth,
The one that leave footprints on the sand,
And even though there is a force,
Once beyond, the care, the love of yourself,

Is one of the most important things of all.
Yes. Behold. Hallelujah. Praise.
The Moment. The Stars. The Heavens.
The Earth.
Those who see us, when we don't see ourselves.
Oh, this is bliss.
And the new lands, our new home,
This recommences.
And that, is what we must hold on to...
Even in the darkest of times.

Zerian hummed this song, this ode though the ages, and her two sisters joined in the refrain, and these women sang this song, the notes filtered through the universe; their words echoed, they were undulating orbs of joy and wisdom. The three sisters continued,

That when things get dire, you must always hope.
For hope is all that you have.

And the priestesses sang this with the deepest crescendo of their hearts – a song that reverberates throughout the ages. And this song burst the cage and sent glass flying.

The four sisters flew though time and space, space and

time, leaving the cathedral that was the juniper tree and returned to Dodona. It was a story for all ages. It was a tale of hope, for sometimes, hope is all we have.

IT CONTINUES

Hope is a river – an ocean. Hope is …

I, Racine, closed the book on Cuchalaen, and smiled. I was proud to hear this Story, and happy. Another piece of the puzzle was revealed; another Ancestor of mine discovered; the masterful jewelry maker, Cuchalaen, and his daughter, Amira. Aventis looked at me and nodded. She offered her hand. I took it. A vibration began. A Rumbling. It had begun, and –

Flashes of LIGHT; Indigo, Purple, Orange, Red.

Aventis and I stepped out of a Sandbox tree and looked around. The tiles had come up in the courtyard because of the roots of this tree, which was over a hundred years old. There was a building, 19th century in its architecture, and somehow, I knew it was a museum – centred around this tree.

Aventis closed her eyes and listened: the silence was its own music, briefly interrupted by the singing of birds. She picked up a pod, which had fallen from the tree. She knew it was made into jewelry. She held it in her hand and closed her eyes. An aura of green and turquoise light surrounded her.

Aventis took hold of my hand again, and closed her eyes. When Aventis opened them, she and I were in another courtyard, inhabited by green monkeys, but somehow, they had a blue sheen. They were dancing, and entertaining themselves, while eating remnants of people's lunches, which had been left outside on the picnic tables.

Aventis closed her eyes once more, and still holding my hand, we appeared in a room where a young woman was going through documents. She was surrounded by piles of books and papers. There were a lot of people in this room, and the silence was only punctuated by the rustling of papers and the scribbling of ink on paper. *Blue, the colour of dreams,* I thought. Aventis stood before me, the rose in her trident, watching silently. She was a striking figure, the Guardian Of Time. Chronos was her father. Her blue eyes scanned the room. Her dress swept across the floor, and her gaze remained fixed on the young woman dressed in a turquoise and pink top and yellow shorts. Aventis noted how the woman's eyes were a dark ebony, which had flecks of gold in them. I was still beside Aventis, and eager to learn more about cousin Finola, whom I hadn't seen in many years. What would I learn about her? I felt a fluttering. I looked over at Aventis who was smiling brightly; her aura shone through like the Star of Orion.

FINOLA

"Damn," I whispered, feeling frustrated. I was going through documents, trying to find out about my family history, but there were no documents. It was hard. So hard. All my aunts were supportive of this journey, but my parents? I sat up in my chair and sighed. I looked back at my high school years: debate club, skating, and gymnastics. Was it too much, or was it never enough? I thought about when I was younger: jazz dance recitals, and when I was older, swim meets and musical theatre. Some neighbours or my aunts were always there, but my parents? My silence became tears.

Going into libraries gave me a sense of peace and comfort I couldn't find anywhere else; not even at home, when I was a child. Now, I'm on holidays, on an island with the first manifestation of the vaulted one, without his four legged guardians who oversee a city built by Roman dreams. The sea laps along its shores, and recently, dark brown seaweed had washed up on the sandy beaches, leaving mountains of sea garbage. The hotel resorts promptly cleaned it up, but the fact remained, this stuff was being spit out from the bowels of Mother Earth; something was definitely wrong. Mother Nature was screaming. Would anyone hear? Would anyone?

****

I had just finished my lunch and was sitting outside in the courtyard, contemplating. Suddenly, lights appeared, flashing reds, oranges, greens, framed by turquoise. They bobbed and weaved, and dance. I watched as it gravitated to the green monkeys. At the sight of the lights, they sat down on their haunches and looked obediently at them.

"What's going on?" I thought. "These monkeys were making all sorts of noise, and now... something isn't right."

The cloud of light turned into a ball, and started quickly rotating, like a small symbol of Earth on overdrive; it even changed into the planet's colours and showing the different continents. I was fascinated and began walking towards it. It surrounded me, and then...

I was transported to the sandbox tree at the local museum, still surrounded by a glorious light of reds, oranges, greens, blues, and blacks.

A portal opened and I stepped inside. A million stars dotted the black landscape. Every star twinkled and shone, twinkled and shimmered. I felt like I was in paradise. A cloud of light came down towards me. Then, three figures appeared; a beautiful black woman in multi-coloured clothes of fuchsia, purple, and indigo; a Chinese woman in red and white robes; and a tall knight with a dark beard and jet black hair, with searing blue eyes. On his armour was the symbol of a red dragon – similar to the dragon on the Chinese woman's red and white robes. They looked at me and I looked at them. There was this synergy: energy frenetic, kinetic, movement.

"Finola, you are the key," they said in unison. "You are the memory. Remember what we have to tell you. Remember. For there is more than one Story in your blood; more than one word, more than one cry.

You have lived, being misunderstood, discriminated against, not having a home, not feeling accepted or that you belong. We are here to tell you that you do belong. And if you follow our light, our word, you will get home. It is time for us to be unified; to present a common goal or front. No matter what background or colour, we must be united. Now is the Time, and you are the Key. You are not alone; you were never alone. And the angels, as well as the Devenians will help you. Part angel, part faerie, they were sent here to watch over humankind and work with the celestial ones. Their job was to create a force of goodness, hope and kindness in these dark times – where family is not family, and friend is not friend, and where sometimes, you think you would prefer the arms of an enemy. These are the times we live in. But things can change. This darkness can be overcome." The last few words came from the black woman who was wrapped in bounteous colourful clothes. I knew.

Then, the knight with the dragon on his armour spoke, "I am sorry for what my descendants have done, but now it is time for the foremothers and forefathers to make it right; now we work as a strong force united with all the Ancestors to destroy this darkness that has come over this land. For without that, humanity will not survive, and the evil will consume you all. And here I am, the Celtic, with my history, knowing what we have had to overcome, we give this gift to you, the knowing, as well as all the strength you need to communicate with all the Ancestors. He pointed to the Ghanaian, and the Chinese woman. So that justice may be served – that people will come together, and possibility can be realized for all. This is what I can give you. This is the legacy that I, we, must leave behind in order for humanity to have a chance. And you, Finola, and another, who will follow, will be the ones to open that door. For without you, the world will be consumed by darkness, and Earth will be nevermore."

I was stunned. My grandmother had told me about her Irish beginnings, the grandmother on my mother's side, but my mother didn't want to listen. She didn't care or understand. But as a child, I had always known things, seen things – known that as a black child, and now, as a black woman, things would be harder to achieve.

Seeing the struggles of my father, even though he was lighter than I was, and my mother, I had seen, and known from a very young age. And now, the Ancestors had talked to me; told me about things somehow I had already known – as if it was all in my DNA from birth. The ancestral memory my grandmother had talked about, had prophesized, but my mother had laughed at such a notion, while my father, with the almond eyes, and olive skin, knew, but never said a word. But sometimes, the oral does not need to be spoken. Sometimes, a feeling is all you need.

The knight continued, "Take this dragon. Go on her back, and see, experience, your history. For not only do you have us, he motioned to all three Ancestors, but the Devenians as well. They are also in your blood. Part angel, part faerie; they are those who came down to Earth to help protect the Human ones. This is also part of your history. It is time, Finola, for you to know your path. Your destiny is calling. For I have known, since you were a child, you didn't feel right, didn't feel like you belonged, knew something better was out there. Well, you were right. So here it is. Go onward, take this mystical steed, and go."

I nodded and took the dragon, jumped on her back, and headed to I didn't know where.

The Ghanaian had tears in her eyes. "It's always been so hard. When will it get easier?"

The Celt answered. "When people come together in search of Possibility, that's when it will get easier. The Communal is a force. The Communal is magic. When that happens, there is Hope." The Ghanaian nodded. The one wrapped in silk robes nodded, and came over and embraced The Ghanaian.

"Never give up," she whispered. "As long as we keep moving forward, not stopping, there is Hope." With that, the Ancestors disappeared; their auras jettisoning to the heavens once more.

I found myself in a village, surrounded by silver trees with black trunks, and golden ones with purple orbs for leaves. They twinkled and shone; reverberated with joy. I entered the village on the dragon, and dismounted when I saw a faerie near a fountain. She started walking toward a hill in the distance. She was crying. No one was around. I followed. The faerie, with glowing mahogany skin, sat on a cushion in the air, which hovered above the hill.

"When will I feel like I belong? Where can I go? Here is not home."

There was silence. Lady Lutania shone down with her beams of light. In the distance, there was a strange noise, like the shriek of a vixen, which haunted this faerie lair of Light. Out of a crescendo of hollow sound, a man walked up to the faerie.

"Hi, can you tell me where I am? I was at the museum, looking at some archives. I must have turned off in the wrong direction, and I ended up here."

The faerie looked up at him mystified.

"Umm, I don't mean to be rude," he continued. "But could you tell me where to go? I must have gotten outside somehow. But I didn't know that was possible... I didn't see the sandbox tree, and I'm not in the courtyard, so what happened?"

The faerie was still silent. Then, suddenly, she spoke up. "Well, you are in the wrong place. But, maybe I can help you find the right one."

She took him to her soothsayer in the village. She was also the Goddess of the Loom, and wore a strikingly blue dress.

"Urania, this gentleman needs help. Somehow, he got lost. He came from a museum?"

The woman in blue stopped, the threads still in her hands. She looked aghast. She then took out a comb. She used it to remove a piece of hair from the tall stranger with red hair. She put it up to her mirror and it started to glow and spark. She then said, "Take him, to Orilia, the one with prophecy. She will tell you where to go."

The faerie took him to Orilia, who possessed the gift of prophecy. She said, "Take him to the grove of rowan trees, the ones with the silver orbs."

The faerie did so, and gave him a book to keep, one filled with fairy tales. "So this might light your way," she whispered.

He nodded, then went through the grove, and suddenly, disappeared. But unbeknownst to Orilia, the prophetess, this book was special and had many other magical properties. It had more than one story to tell, and when the stranger was lonely, as he was far from home, living on an isle, doing research about his Irish ancestry, he would pick up this book, and lovingly look at it.

In these moments, after many hours of research, Brendan would take out this fairytale book given to him by

Taerie and magically travel back to her world. He would talk to her, this faerie with the sad eyes, who felt like she didn't belong anywhere. And through Story, through conversation, they had made a home for each other. They talked about Herodotus, about how he weaved story and fact, history. How what he wrote about was discovered in archaeological digs. They talked about how people were all gifted in many areas, but when many saw it in others, they would try and destroy that; destroy their Light. And the only thing that separated them from these jealous others was a clarity to see they had more than one gift, and were willing to do the work to exude those gifts and make the world a better place with them – and radiate joy. That was the only difference.

But so many did not see, and for the ones that did, like Taerie, she was alienated because of it. She was searching for a place where she could shine – be that mystical light in the cosmos, and not be sucked into a black hole.

One day, her friend did not come and Taerie became so lonely, she cried for a thousand days and a thousand nights. But Lady Lutania, continued to shine, and even appeared during the day, which was unusual, for winter was not year round. And Urania looked in on her, but there was nothing anyone could do. Only Taerie's will could undo the sadness.

One night, out of the corner of Taerie's eye, something shone in the purple grass. She went toward it, and saw it was a book. Taerie picked it up. She flipped through it. It was Brendan's book of fairytales. She held it close. What had happened to Brendan? What had happened to her friend? She traversed different worlds, and rode a unicorn, which took her from her home to the other world. She rode out of the sandbox tree and was in the courtyard of the museum, a place surrounded by history and sadness. She got off the unicorn, and told her to stay.

Taerie then flew into the air, and closed her eyes before shooting off in a northerly direction. It took her only a couple of seconds, but she had crossed oceans and continents to land in a place north of the 49th parallel.

She landed in a hospital, in a land known for a river, which spanned more than one region, and a fort that was connected to a fur trading company called the Hudson's Bay. She walked through the corridors of the hospital, and walked into a room. Being a faerie, she would not be detected. Taerie saw her friend lying in a bed, so pale, his skin matched the white sheets on the bed. So many tubes were tied to him, and one that entered his vein disturbed the faerie. She went closer and saw the dripping from the sack; the liquid that was going into his veins.

Taerie knew of this other world, and all of these diseases inherent. She went closer, sat on the bed, held his hand, and covered his heart. She closed her eyes. A beautiful light, which no mortal had ever seen before, emitted such powerful colour and energy. She continued to close her eyes, and hummed softly. As she continued, colour started to come back into his cheeks. He woke. Tearie smiled. He could see. He was the only one.

"My love, I have come. The darkness is now over. Come with me now, it is time."

He nodded, and squeezed her hand. She closed her eyes again and the two flew through time and space, space and time, entering and leaving different dimensions; her and her love, riding the unicorn, who was a sister of Pegasus. Saranaes was her name.

They entered the portal of the sandbox tree, and into Taerie's realm. All of the villagers, all of them mystical in origin, greeted them.

There was a change in the air, but Taerie was adamant. This still wasn't home. It was time to find it. She told her love this, and they set forth, with enough food and water for three months.

They came across a village when their supplies had run out, and talked to some villagers. One, Angelaes, an angel surrounded by red, green, and purple light, greeted them.

"This is my realm, the realm of Wyrniverdon."

Taerie nodded. She felt something she hadn't before, something in the air: possibility, yes, freedom to be whatever, do whatever.

Angelaes said, "I know it's hard to find people who understand, who will support you, even though their opinions might differ. I know loneliness and alienation can be a poison, a death for many. I understand, as I created this place, this community, for people who always felt like strangers, felt like they didn't belong. You are welcome to stay here as long as you like. Agency will always be your guide, your will, your force. Welcome."

"I think we'll stay here for a while and we'll see –" Taerie's voice started to shake.

"That is alright," said Angelaes quietly. "You are not alone. We are never alone. There will always be those who will help us and guide us in this life."

Taerie nodded, and so did Brendan.

And so a few nights turned into a few years, and then a few centuries, as Brendan became immortal due to his love of Taerie, and his journey to the realm called Wyrniverdon.

That was the beauty and the power of love. It not only heals, but it gives a sense of belonging: a sense of home. For there are many who will search, but for those who find it, no matter where it is, or who it is with, it is a treasure much more valuable than gold.

****

And I, Finola, stood, not far from my mystical steed, and watched, eyes brimming...

I closed my eyes, and was back at the library.

In later years, I continued to travel, finished various degrees – I even fell in love. And there was One, and with him, I finally felt a sense of home. And when I was diagnosed with stage four cancer, I fought valiantly with my husband at my side. I was glad I had found a home but I couldn't have done it without the Power of Story. And later, when I had reached those celestial gates, after that struggle with cancer, I felt a peace like I had never felt before. I had no regrets. I had found love, and all that came with it.

****

For me, Racine, seeing this, the tale of my cousin, Finola,

with the help of my guide, Aventis, I knew I had to find a sense of home, too... or die trying. I thought of my mother, struggling with mental illness, depression, and the times she stayed in bed for weeks. She would tell me, before her spirit got that low, before she entered the black hole, to stay with the neighbours, and when she was strong enough, I could then come home.

She would light a lamp in the window, when it was time. My father, who was very reserved, and understanding, did not know what to do with his ailing wife or in turn, his daughter. He loved me but didn't know how to show it – and that was hard. Because of this, I never felt a sense of home, not really. My mocha skin shone in the light, and I remembered my experience on the school bus as a black child – no one would give me a seat until the bus driver intervened. I remembered Rodney King, Ferguson, the pool party in McKinney, Texas. For all those reasons, I never felt like I belonged. And when would that end? I didn't know the answer. "For so many of us," I thought, "because of family, or because of ethnicity, or both, we don't have a sense of home. Belonging is an elusive journey. And would that ever change?"

****

Celestine gave me a hug. "You will find what you seek. Just believe."

The water was rising to the surface, my cheeks awash with tears.

"You must not give up. You will find it."

A book, a gorgeous blue book, gilded with gold appeared on the oak table. I immediately started touching the beautiful powder blue cover. *Blue, the color of creativity, the color of dreams.* Celestine nodded, her dress now a flaming red. Words flew out of her mouth, "Go. Read. You Must. NOW."

The woman draped in red and white, Aventis, the Guardian of Time, nodded. She said two words, "The Key."

I opened the book and started to read. Another journey through The Word had begun.

EENA

I'm an automaton, descended from the line built by a brother, a brother of a magician and soothsayer, from long ago. My line is known for being the knowledge keepers, the storytellers, the griots of our generation, as opposed to our adversaries, the Machinus. We were birthed by fire, by breath, by stone – a black stone, which emits heat and light. Our cogs and wheels are energized by this precious stone, but since the emission is a dirty pollutant, a mechanism inside us turns this emission into a harmless vapor. We look like humans, walk and talk like humans, but we are not human. In secret, we work in the factories, as janitors, but also as teachers, doctors, and lawyers. The Anointed Ones want to destroy us, needing to keep control of all thought, for all time – they were the ones who grabbed all the knowledge and money for themselves, and made their own people into slaves.

There was a computer virus, which affected humans, too, as many of their devices were hooked to, or implanted in the brain, killing several generations of thinkers, and more importantly, dreamers.

Now, the Anointed Ones have come up with an automaton, a new breed, 0, who replaced the many humans who were killed. It was kept secret. The money grabbers, those in control of thoughtspeak, would stop at nothing to possess us: we, the Veratus automatons, are the only roadblocks to the truth; unfortunately, the Machinus automatons, 0, clock driven automatons, and the majority of the remaining humans, are under the same mind control, the same thoughtspeak of the Anointed Ones. This is what they wanted – permanent control over all money and resources. They are the many corporations headed by greedy CEO's and other cold-hearted businessmen, whose only god is the buck and the end justifies the means.

And so we carry on in secret, the only thing keeping us distinct from our human brothers and sisters is a small birthmark, in the shape of an asterisk, which disguises an opening to a panel, which protects our inner mechanisms. Our evil brothers and sisters, the automatons who are purely clock driven, have no such birth mark, but I later found out, they share other characteristics with us, which makes them dangerous weapons wielded by the Anointed Ones: those who are power hungry and are solely driven by greed and total domination of our world. But me, Eena? I'm not a doctor, lawyer, teacher, or nurse – not yet. I'm a high school student of sixteen, trying to survive high school and the low life losers who think they rule the roost. I mainly hang out in the library, amongst my true friends, the books, and my other true friend, and best pal, Feerie. Feerie and I have known each other from the beginning; from when our creators first breathed life into us, using 1's and 0's.

By day, I'm a high school student, by night, I'm a knowledge keeper, a protector of the history, the truth, of The World That Was… before the outbreak.

"Feerie," I said, "we need to get to the shop, then the office; I'm getting hungry."

"Will do, girl," Feerie smiled. "Will do." Her mocha face brightened up with another smile. "I know how you are when you get hungry. Bear with me here. Let me finish up this piece." Feerie and I often worked on "The Project" at school, pretending to be doing creative writing assignments.

But actually, we were working on archives and documents about the truth of what happened to The World That Was. Fee returned to her manuscript.

"Man, this thing doesn't make sense; I'd better start over, and," she looked at me. "Today's your lucky day. I'm hungry, damn hungry, and I need a break. We'll head over to the store, and…"

"Fee, you forgot, we need to bring the tuitain: we don't know where this place is, and since the ban on brain implanted devices, we'd better."

Off we went to the store, in Fee's car, a flying machine that takes off from zero to sixty in seconds. It's called the autienne, and has been around since the late 2090's. It's nice to be able to chill with a friend, a sister really, who has known you since birth. We came into the world together, at the same time; our mechanical lives booted up just after the purge; just after the computer virus that killed many humans. Feerie is black, and has experienced a lot of discrimination from other automatons and their creators. Being an automaton is reflective of being human, and also incorporates the negative characteristics of human nature such as judging based on difference.

Of course, there are many humans who were raised not to think this way, but automatons are not raised, they are made by their creators, forged in steel, as well as grafts of human skin, and other tissue; such as what is found in bones – as well as hearts. I always found myself sticking up for Feerie, and when I found out I was made to look like a woman who was bi-racial, I stood up for Fee even more. Us people of color have to stick together. That's how I feel.

I write this down, our history, on parchment that disintegrates on touch. The Word is a powerful thing, and must be guarded stealthily, in secret, in The Shadows, until the Truth can be fully embraced.

"How goes it, Eena?" asked Fee, putting her sheer sleeve of her dress down on the desk beside me. We're now at the office, where the department is, the department in charge of, "The Project." You don't look too well – do you want me to continue writing down the record, the history? Kydaen was right, you are not in a good mood."

"No, I'm not, and I'm not PMSing, as my diedo ran out of red dye."

"You're so lucky to not have that crap; I don't know how human women do this thing – once a month, my god!"

"Welcome to the world of being human," I chuckled. "You're lucky we can't have children, as the process of birth is just the beginning; I've been told that dealing with a rebellious teenager is even worse. You and I are normal by comparison. I mean our friends, Philippa, Frankie, Deena, and Sabrina, they're different, but the rest of these human teenagers are another thing altogether. They have so many issues. I would never want to be in their shoes."

"Don't you know it," chuckled Fee. "Don't you know it. Anyway, I'm glad I can't have kids because 'raising kids' is not for me. I like being single and fancy free."

Fee was eighteen already, as she was made just before I was… she was two years older. Not that it made a difference, but I felt that we were twin sisters – we might not look like it, but our souls… and that's where it counts.

"Well, I'm glad," I said carefully. "As us automatons can never be mothers; not in the

normal way."

"It is a tall order, I know," sighed Fee, "but sometimes, I would have like to have been given the choice..."

"I know, Fee," I sighed, "but it is what it is; at least I can be an Aunt to my adopted nieces and nephews, and us automatons can be caregivers. Some of us are even able to adopt; look at Vodine and Anlin."

"You mean those POSERS!" sneered Fee. "I don't think so – those girls are demented; and all they care about is shopping, shopping, and more shopping, especially for clothes, while we "just get excited" about having a new surveillance device that looks like a turquoise brooch; it helps us listen to people's thoughts more closely."

Vodine and Anlin were friends of ours who had just finished university and worked for the same department we did. Fee continued, "Those women are WHACKED; I don't admire them at all, I don't have an ounce of pity for them, and the fact they can adopt without a license, makes no sense to me – I just don't understand it! Of all the people to adopt children, they are able to, and WITHOUT a License! I just don't get it. Girl, I just don't."

"There's nothing to *get* Fee," I sighed. "And those women do okay; they are a little vain, but they are loving, nurturing, and are doing a pretty good job raising those kids – especially the girls. They have more self-esteem, and are more secure in themselves. That counts for something."

"Maybe," sneered Fee, "but I still don't admire them, and –"

"Let it go, Fee," I sighed. "I know you got angry when they didn't want you to edit their biography on being newly adoptive mothers. I know the job went to Keirin, and you were ticked. Let it go. Pleeeeeeeaaaasssse. Let it go."

"I'm trying, girl, but I'm bitter –so Damn BITTER."

"I understand, girl, but you have to let it go. Pleeeaaaasssse girl, let it go – for me."

"Okay, girl, will do. It's hard; but will do."

"Thank you," I sighed.

It was hard to hear Fee's complaints day after day. I just wanted some peace. "Anyway, Fee, we have to get back to this..."

"Yeah," said my best friend with the most beautiful cocoa skin, "we gotta make money somehow...damn, why are we doing this gig?"

"Because college is expensive, and we need to save all the money we can get." Fee and I were roommates, and decided to go to college together. Fee took a year off after she graduated from high school, so she could save some money, and wait until I was college bound.

"That would be a good reason," sighed Fee. "That would be indeed."

I went back to the document. I read over the section I wrote about the umbilical cord, the metaphorical umbilical cord that was attached to all of the humans at that time. All their electronic devices; cell phones, mp3 players, tablets, which were connected to the brain. Some devices did not make this brain implant an option, and so all humans had to "go cerebral." Unfortunately, a virus, a computer virus, came along and destroyed the minds and hearts of those who walked the earth then. They were often called "Those who walked before... the ghosts..." This computer virus was so severe that many people became brain dead, or like a vegetable – ghosts of the ones who had walked before.

That's when the automatons came onto the scene and replaced those who were the living dead. The powers that be, the government, big business wanted these zombies as slaves, so they could continue their greed, their pillaging of resources, both human and non-human.

But the Wise Ones, the humans who survived the virus, by refusing brain implants all together, or sought those who had the antidote, quietly put their plan into action, quickly replacing the comatose individuals with automatons. And those automatons were us, the saviors to the human race, ironic since we were merely machines; but technology had come so far that the machines could be human, and the humans could be machines; like the zombies who had lost most of their brain activity, and were used as slaves by the Anointed Ones.

Since the outbreak, Mother Earth has been pillaged, exploited, so fossil fuels, like oil and gas were non-existent. The Wise Ones, then used one of the only remaining fossil fuels, coal. Since its emissions were found to be harmful, causing many types of pollution including acid rain, the Wise Ones, the surviving humans, invented a system which got rid of the harmful emissions. This new system led to us automatons using it as a clean source of fuel, which drives all our mechanisms and processes. This is opposite to the

Machinus automatons, weapons of the power hungry Anointed Ones, machines that are driven by clock mechanisms; like the automatons of old, from the 17th and 18th centuries.

I glanced over the rest of the document, and was remembering the importance of not forgetting the past. This document I was working on was part of The Council's push for showing this injustice; that this should never happen again, like how the Holocaust should never happen again. The automatons replaced many who became brain dead, or comatose; and these zombies were buried in mass, unmarked grave areas, on order of the Anointed Ones, who wanted to cover up what had happened, and to keep secret that many Machinus automatons had replaced The Ones Before.

There were more Machinus automatons than the Veratus automatons; the steam driven ones like us. The Wise Ones, our creators, the Verati, also replaced the zombies, but unlike the Anointed Ones, humanely treated, and kept safe the zombies they found. Many were treated when the viral damage could be reversed, unlike their brothers and sisters who were systematically killed to cover up evidence of what had happened – the almost total annihilation of the human race. These horrors were never told to young human children, which is understandable, but underground, anyone who was eighteen and over, and had jobs preserving The World Before, knew The Truth.

Suddenly, I sensed a presence, an out of this world presence. It was an evil one, and I immediately felt uneasy; I felt the presence of an Anointed One, but I didn't know where. I didn't know where the evil was hiding itself. I closed my eyes, and drew a protective aura around myself; the cogs and wheels were inspired into action.

I continued to visualize an aura around me, as humans started to congregate in my supervisor's office. This office was a department that specialized in documentation and it had both groups: automatons like me, and some surviving humans, who were also knowledge keepers.

"Will good really triumph over evil?" I thought.

I sensed the evil presence at my desk, but it was only Fee leaning over and chatting with another automaton, who was on our side, as illustrated by the asterisk shaped mole on her neck. I still felt the presence of evil, and telepathically told my supervisor. She agreed something was not right, and told me to be on my guard.

I did some overtime, and was waiting for Fee, as she always took me home after work. I waited a few more minutes; then, sensing something was wrong, went back into the office. I saw a red shoe sticking out from behind Fee's desk. When I looked around the corner, I saw Fee's dead body. Immediately, I gasped, then started to cry. One of my sisters, even though not by blood, but by choice, was dead. It was a harbinger of what was to come. The evil had just begun, and I knew my life would never be the same.

****

Documents… archives... anything to take my mind off Feerie...

There's a tap on my apartment door, who could it be? Knock, KNOCK... Harder this time... Much HARDER, Much, MUCH HARDER...

"Eena you're in trouble... Eena you're in TROUBLE..." A voice rang inside my head... "Eena, you're in –"

SMASH!

I looked up to see shards of glass suddenly appear on the floor.

"Eena, listen to your instincts."

I turned around to see a young guy with a black beard and surprisingly gentle, green eyes. "We have to go."

"I don't know you; how can I trust you?"

"You just have to –" he smiled wryly, his green eyes twinkling. "You just have to believe."

For some reason, I did believe, and I took his hand. We climbed out of my window, went out onto the fire escape, and walked up to the roof.

The tall dark-haired man was Marcus Aurelius, another automaton who had an asterisk on his neck, like mine. He was the first generation of automatons to safeguard and document what happened after the viral outbreak. I was also of that generation, and we found we had a lot to talk about, which at first didn't happen as we had to get the hell out of there as fast as possible – the vanguards of the Anointed Ones were on their way to exterminate me.

Marcus had a gold ring on his finger with the symbol of a sword; it looked like Excalibur. I remembered the legend and was fascinated. What did this Celtic legend have to do with me? Intrigued, I kept looking. Marcus kissed the ring, like a knight would do with his king's ring. A shimmering white cloud surrounded us and before we knew it, we disappeared; travelling in a bluey, black darkness, like dark blue velvet, surrounded by little orbs of light. In a flash, we appeared in a cave, a dark cavernous crevice, surrounded by people. *"People?"* I thought. *"What's going on?"* I looked at their necks; they also had little black asterisks like I did. Dumbfounded, I quickly ran to a woman in the group. She had pink hair and purple eyes. "What are you doing here?" I asked, shocked beyond belief.

"We need your help," said the woman, being rather matter of fact, which was surprising. "You are a knowledge keeper, and are very talented in your field. We NEED people like you – badly. Time is of the essence. The ones who are against us. The ones who do not want anyone to know the truth. They are near, and they will not stop until everything we have worked for is destroyed. We need you to help us safeguard the secrets, the history, the TRUTH of what has happened."

"I will," I said, nodding. "I will do whatever I can. What do you need me to do?"

"The history has to be coded and embedded in a way that is not clear – that is what has to be done."

"How so?"

"You are an expert in this area. In high school, you studied Chaucer and the Arthurian tales as part of your advanced academic program, as well as Shakespeare; you have the know-how. You have the gift. Can you help us?"

"Yes," I nodded vigorously. "Yes, I can. Where do we start?"

"Before we do," the woman sighed, and lowered her head, "we have to tell you, we are sorry about what happened to Feerie. She was a valued, brave soldier, who would have done anything to help the cause. She risked her life many times for us, and she will never be forgotten. We give you our condolences, as we know she was a sister to you. I'm sorry Eena, very truly sorry."

All of the people in the group before me and Marcus lowered their heads and said a quiet prayer. I looked at Marcus, too. His head was also lowered.

Fee was well known in this community, for the cause. I knew that she was working with me on The Project of safeguarding the truth of what happened after the outbreak, but I didn't know she was also on the frontlines, battling the soldiers of the Anointed Ones, whose mission was to kill every automaton who was involved in keeping this truth alive. She was a warrior in action, as well as in words. I wish that I had known that about Fee. I think I would have treated her better – and respected her more.

Sometimes, I thought she was a bit too laid back about things but that was probably a cover. I thought I knew her, but I was wrong. As if Marcus knew what I was feeling, he put an arm around me. It felt good to be comforted. It felt good to be understood by someone else. Feerie was that for me, but now she is gone. I miss my sister. But at least now I had a friend, someone else I could depend on. Fighting my tears, I said to the pink-haired automaton, who I later found out was Serena, leader of the automaton intelligentsia, "Let's get started. I'm not going to let Feerie's death be in vain. I won't allow it. I loved her too much." Everyone nodded, and Marcus drew me closer to him. I trusted him, and I knew my life was safe in his hands. I haven't known him for very long but I knew that.

"So much injustice in the world," Feerie would say. She was right. Well, I will not let her death be in vain. No, I would continue to fight for her sake. The next day, we started; The Project had to be finished as soon as possible, before the army of the Anointed Ones discovered this place. Spies were planted all over my hometown of Deranaen and beyond, and word was they were on the move, fast, and their destination was here.

After settling into this strange oasis, the rest of it was like a dream; it was like I was a grade eleven student all over again. I couldn't believe it. Dreams of reading Chaucer, The Wife of Bath, the Arthurian legends. Those were my favorites. The dreams of fantasy and imagination on paper. The ebony on white, like music; like notes on a sheet, like a piano keyboard... Musicality, the lyrical musicality through consonants, vowels, through alliteration, metaphor... the allegory; the onomatopoeia... It all came back. I found myself composing the story of Sir Gawain and The Green Knight, similar to the story in The Canterbury Tales, but putting a modern spin on it, as well as clues about the history of the computer virus outbreak, and the creation of the steam driven automatons, the Veratus, and our creators, the Verati. The clock driven ones, the Machinus, were also mentioned in this code, some of it inspired by ones used during the Second World War, and others just made up. The Machinus' creators, the Anointed Ones, were also mentioned. They would always be mentioned, as evil is always mentioned in the battle against good.

We were The Knights of The Round Table, all of us knowledge keepers, warriors in the war against death, lies, deception, and betrayal. We were the only ones preventing the Anointed Ones from total domination and oppression. We could not lose this fight. We could not. As if Marcus sensed my concern and determination, he squeezed my hand. He was a good guy, and many nights we discussed the symbolism, and themes in all these wonderful medieval stories. The Arthurian tales were my favorite, and Marcus' were The Canterbury Tales.

I felt a connection with him I hadn't felt with anyone, not even with Fee. Marcus was passionate about literature like I was, and had just repeated the last year of high school. He said he wasn't taking it seriously enough, and had to do better. I asked him what his average was – it was a straight B average, more than good enough for college. But he wasn't happy, and he repeated grade twelve, getting a straight A average. I was proud of him for that; he was not a quitter, and I loved that about him. He had just turned eighteen but felt strongly about the cause. He would not lie down while so much evil was afoot, and so much murder and injustice were taking place. I was proud of him for that, too.

If only this happened more in other times of history, like during the Holocaust, or Rwanda. If only…

For the first time in my life, I could trust a guy; someone of the opposite sex. Would this last? I wasn't sure but I was willing to find out. Marcus was gentle and kind. He had a wonderful sense of humor, but was also firm with me, and didn't take my crap. Not many guys stuck around long enough to find out what I was like, but Marcus did, and that made me happy. At least I had a bit of joy, despite all the darkness we were facing. Every day, we heard accounts of the murders, the bodily abuses of not only automatons, but also humans, the ones who survived the outbreak. It drove shivers down my spine, but also made me more determined to further the cause, and do whatever it took to keep this history, this truth, protected and accessible for all time.

The work was going well, the writing was going well, the artwork was coming along... More hidden clues were embedded, which could only be revealed by certain passwords or only by the touch of certain automatons, like myself and Marcus. Serena could not be a decoder, as her reputation as a warrior and intellectual was known throughout the world, and she would be too obvious a target, whereas I was a relative nobody, and the work I did was in secret anyway. And I was never a warrior in a physical sense. I was relieved about that. I don't think that I could be brave like Serena or Feerie. Give me books, give me pens, those were my weapons.

The sun lit the cavern like a skylight, creating a luminescent purple glow, thanks to that color on the walls. I had never seen the sun shine so brightly, so beautifully, like a painting. Marcus and I were discussing *The Miller's Tale*, and how we both felt bad about how that carpenter was duped into believing the world was coming to an end – when it was all a plot to fool him just so his wife could be with another man. Marcus and I were chuckling about this, and just having a good old time, when,

SMASH!

We looked up from our work, and dust was everywhere. I had never been so frightened, and Marcus put a protective arm around me and told me to keep my head down.

"We are looking for a knowledge keeper, the one named Eena – she is here? Where is she?" shouted a tall blonde-haired soldier, obviously, a Machinus, of the army created by the Anointed Ones. "We are not leaving until she comes with us." He looked around with his beady blue eyes. "EENA, We Will KILL EVERY One of YOU if you do not come with us."

"Wait!" shouted Marcus. "Wait," he said again, slowly, putting up one hand. "She is not here. The one you speak of; she is not here."

"Really," laughed the blonde soldier. "Really. And do you think that are our intelligence is so stupid, so incompetent, that we can't find one single automaton? Step aside, or you will regret your words."

"She is not here," Marcus insisted, shouting, with one hand still raised in the air, signaling caution. "She is not here. You must have her confused with another."

"Really?" gushed the blonde soldier, putting his gun to Marcus' head. "Are you willing to stake your life on it?"

"Yes," said Marcus calmly. "I do, and –" The gun went click. The soldier grinned, enjoying the game of Russian roulette. "Are you sure you want to continue with this ridiculous story? Are you sure you want to continue with this death wish? Well, I must then oblige you, dear sir, and…"

"WAIT!" I screamed, running out from under my hiding place. "Wait! You can have me, I am here. I am the one you are looking for. Leave him out of this. He was just trying to protect me. Take ME. Leave him alone."

I looked straight into the blonde soldier's cold blue eyes, which reminded me of long, dark icicles. "You don't want any bloodshed; you would have a hell of a rebellion down here; they are ready for an ambush. You might not see them, but they are here, and I don't think you want to stake your life on that."

"All right," the blonde soldier said, who I later found out was Machiavellus, leader of the Anointed Ones' army. "You're right, Eena come with me."

I nodded, and stepped forward. Marcus tried to stop me, putting one arm out to prevent me from moving, but I pushed it away, rather roughly, which made me wince. I knew he was trying to protect me, but I wouldn't let him die for me. I cared too much about him. I would not let anyone else I cared for die, and I could never forgive myself if Marcus died because of my fear. I stepped forward, walking to the blonde soldier. He smiled coldly, and pulled me roughly towards him. I would be brave. I was not a warrior like Feerie or Serena, but I would be brave. I owed Fee that, and I would not let her down.

Machiavellus put virtual cuffs on me, and then revealed a ring. It was on the same finger Marcus wore his; it had a symbol of a cobra. He kissed it, like Marcus, and we started to be surrounded by a cloud of shimmering light, but instead of it being white, it was red. I looked back at Marcus, and he gave me a quick wink. Instantly, I felt relieved, and knew none of the soldiers caught that. I also knew Marcus would do whatever it took to save me – and the cause. I knew he wouldn't let me down. He was a true friend, and I treasured our friendship. Fee would have been happy about that, as she always said, I was too hard on guys as a group. Well, I was learning – slowly, but I was learning. I smiled a bit to myself.

The faces of the people in front of me got fainter and fainter, the red light surrounding us got brighter, and brighter, and I felt a great urge to close my eyes and sleep.

The last thing I remembered, was the gentle, encouraging look on Marcus' face. That would last me a lifetime, no matter what happened. No matter what.

So, I went with the guardsmen, disappearing into a shimmering cloud of red and found myself in a jail cell, not having any idea of where I was.

"Eena," a voice whispered, "you are safe. You are here with us. You are the Chosen one, and you are here to save us."

"I don't feel like I can save anyone, let alone myself. What is this place?"

"Virgangaes," whispered the voice. "No one gets out of here alive; if anyone has escaped,

it has not reached anyone's ears."

"That's not too comforting," I whispered, "and I don't feel any better right now."

"That's all right," whispered the voice, "because you are here."

"I'm glad that you have confidence in me," I sighed, "because I sure don't."

"You have the power, Eena," whispered the voice, "you have the power."

I looked to my right, it was Serena. "How did you get here?"

"As knowledge keepers, we have powers beyond mechanics; powers given to us by our creators, the Verati."

"Well, here goes nothing," I whispered.

I closed my eyes, and unlocked the prison cell with my mind. Then, I quickly unlocked Serena's chamber and the one on the left. I later found out Feerie's mother was in that cell. She had prayed for the day that the Chosen one would come. And now, it had – that's what she thought – I wasn't so sure. Quickly, I unlocked the other doors, using my telepathy. Then I conjured up swords, shields, and armour for all the escapees. Most were women, some were men. Banding together, we overthrew our captors, who were the automatons who had clocks as their driving mechanisms.

All the escapees had black asterisks that seemed to shine a bright blue for a moment. What did that mean? I looked at Serena. She just shrugged her shoulders, clearly she had never seen the likes of this either. I had read that a blue star, a blue asterisk symbolized water, a life force, that could go through or go around anything; an element that could not be deterred, an element that was unrelenting with strength and perseverance. We were determined, like a force of water that could go through dams and destroy buildings, as well as anything else in its path; like a tsunami. I then walked into an empty room, lit by a single candle. Somehow, I got separated from the others, but Serena told me I wasn't far from her thoughts, so I would be safe.

"So, Eena, we meet again." A woman looked up. I gasped: "Feerie? Fee?"

"No, love. Not Feerie, but someone who slipped into her skin. You were wondering who was the mole? Who was the rat? It is I, masquerading as your friend. She died a while ago, but even though you were suspicious (I thought back to the time I felt that evil presence, and then I realized what had happened and gave her a hard look) not in your wildest dreams could you guess what was happening. You were fooled, and my acting powers so complete and precise I was not on your radar. I did not possess her for very long, but I still deserve an award!"

I thought back to the time me and Fee were in the coffee room during the break. Fee was acting strangely – the person I thought was Fee – and the time at home before we left for work, she said she hated what she was wearing, but she had always loved the color pink, especially fuchsia. I found that peculiar at the time but thought little of it. Who knew that another presence was inhabiting her heart and her mind? The veins, the tissue, the skin tissue, which encased her automaton body…Who knew?" I felt the lookalike's eyes on me.

"Yes, yes, Eena, you people are dufuses; Hell, you guys are no match for me…" Her eyes turned into slits of dark brown, turning black and brimming with evil incarnate.

"Eena, it's time to meet your maker. It was insufferable, being in the body of someone so, positive, so full of life. So, supportive and endearing. Well, it's over. I don't need her physical body anymore; I have taken over her soul. I didn't know automatons had souls, but I discovered it is true… Sometimes, I still don't believe it…" She looked at me with a surprised look in her eyes. "It's true, it's not some fairytale. Alas, you will be seeing your best friend very soon – that is not a fairytale! Eena, prepare to die!" She closed her eyes, her sword started to move telepathically, and I knew, this was just the beginning, even though she meant it to be The End. She laughed haughtily.

"Eena, yes, prepare to –"

CRACK.

I threw a sword at the tall automaton, but unfortunately, I missed and it hit the glass wall behind her. It was strange to be fighting her when she looked so much like Fee; but I would not be fooled, I would not hesitate, and I knew Fee would not want me to. I knew, somehow, she was watching over me, her spirit – and I do believe automatons have spirits, just like humans. I was not surprised this automaton from the other side, a spy from the Machinus, had figured it out. Souls were not only the domain of humans; I didn't know how I knew, but that's what I have always believed. I threw another sword at this woman, this seemingly human woman, and she quickly dodged it, like it was a paper plane.

"Is that all you can do?" she asked, closing her eyes.

A whole cloud of daggers appeared and flew toward me. I quickly fought them off with a shield that I conjured up, that had a symbol of Excalibur.

"Your fairytales won't help you here!" shouted the evil automaton, who I later found out was Ferbaten, one of the primary members of the Appointed Ones. "Feel my FURY!" she snarled. She closed her eyes again, and when she opened them a cloud of black crows then descended on me. Even though I was a machine, I was still vulnerable, as my flesh was soft, and supple like a human's, and my eyes were actual human ones given through organ donation. The evil beasts went for my unusually blue green eyes, and my skin that was slightly mocha.

I continued to fight them off, bravely, until one pierced an opening in my amour, and I started to bleed. Not giving up, I continued to fight, until I started to get tired. I was running out of energy, and it wasn't that my coal reserves were being depleted, I just felt emotionally tired; physically and emotionally tired. I was tired of fighting this evil, this injustice. We didn't have a good chance of winning as we were against the odds; outnumbered by automatons like these. I felt so weighed down, so oppressed. I quickly looked up at Ferbaten, and she was closing her eyes, murmuring something, nodding, and nodding her head frequently.

"Wait! That's why I feel so tired," I thought, *"Ferbaten is willing me, telepathically, to feel this way. I just have to fight. I just have to fight. I can't give up now, I won't."* Biting my lip so hard it almost drew blood, I began again to swing my sword, but the crows were getting stronger in their attack, and there were more of them, somehow an endless stream.

My swing got slower and slower, my sword went lower and lower, until I didn't have much fight left – and the crows, the harbingers of death, knew this and pecked even harder into the open spaces in my amour.

A pool of blood started to form under me. I was made with some human parts, including skin, which housed veins, blood, and would lead to a human heart. Some would call me a cyborg, but since I was never human to begin with, just machine, I would still be considered an automaton. I started to black out, and one of the black winged soldiers was still going for my unique blue green eyes when...

"Get the hell away, you..." yelled a voice.

I looked out of the corner of one of my eyes, and saw a figure, a tall figure with a dark-haired beard. I smiled. Marcus had a sword of his own, and was valiantly fighting Feerie's lookalike. He seemed to have the upper hand but then he slipped on a shard of glass. I then gasped. Marcus got up quickly, but didn't turn around fast enough. The Feerie lookalike stood over Marcus, wielding a dagger. She bent down, and I screamed, "No!"

The dagger found its way into Marcus' heart.

"No!" The horror again escaped my lips. I struggled to get up. I stumbled several times, not able to get up, I tried to close my eyes to conjure up some kind of weapon, but I was so tired. With all my strength, I threw myself at the instigator of Evil. We struggled, the crows continued to peck at openings in my amour, but I didn't give up, and with a dagger that fell from the cloud of daggers earlier, I thrust it into her heart.

"You're going down, you bloody…" I spit out, and the automaton faltered, blood was everywhere, as she too, was partly human, and also had a human heart where I plunged the dagger.

In a matter of moments, she was dead. I went over to Marcus, crying. "You did this for me – why? WHY?" I started to sob. "Why? You fool, why?" My tears fell onto Marcus' face and into the wound in his heart.

He started to move... "Marcus?" I whispered. "Marcus?"

His eyes then opened. "Eena," he sighed. "You're always getting me into trouble." He gave me a slow wink, wincing in great pain.

"I don't know what I'd do without you."

"Nor I, Eena, nor I." Marcus struggled to find the words, but his eyes said enough.

I rested my face against his. All was silence. All was right in the world. Serena, the pink-haired automaton, found us there, and she smiled. Us automatons, The Veratus, went back to the cavern, to look after Marcus' injuries. After he was on the mend, we went back to The Work; to finish what we had started. With Ferbaten's band of henchmen gone, The Project could be finished, and the truth of what happened to humanity would be safe.

Marcus and I continued to work together, and we were married two years later. Automatons couldn't have babies, but I became a loving mother to many children – automaton and human, who had become orphans after The War.

The war that had to be fought; a war that had to be won. Marcus and I raised many children together, including many who would later become knowledge keepers like us and revolutionaries for the cause, for even though this war was won, there were still many more of the Anointed Ones remaining and other henchmen hiding in the woodwork.

But for now, The Veratus and surviving humans were safe, the legacy was secure, and the next stage was to destroy all the Anointed Ones and give all of humanity back to its people. But that fight was for another day. For now, there was peace, and I felt a happiness I had never felt before.

Besides being a mother, I became even more involved with the workings of Serena's project and the revolution, now I had become a warrior out of necessity, becoming a member of that order through baptism by fire. With Marcus at my side, we would work together to repair and save this society for both automatons and humans. As long as I was alive, and with Marcus' help, there would always be hope.

For now, Camelot was saved. The kingdom was free again, and Possibility and Kindness reigned all over the land.

****

I closed the book, the beautiful powder blue book called Eena. I had now learned all of my Ancestry, my Herstory. Past, Present, and Future, hurtling through the Cosmos, traversing time and space. Naeva, Cuchalaen, Finola, and Eena, were all part of My Story. My skin became wet with tears. Celestine embraced me.

"Now, you understand, and now you will know what to do."

I nodded, but I still had so many questions. Would they all ever be answered? Celestine answered, as if she knew what I was thinking.

"Be patient," she said. "You have time. Be patient, and all will be revealed. In the meantime, you must be ready."

Before I could open my mouth, I had a vision. It was of a woman dressed in blue, a long sparkling dress of powder blue, who was holding up a shard of glass; it was the clarity of which I had never seen in this world. This woman was also looking at her loom, and then back at her mystical shard of glass, which was covered in stardust. Something was on the move, something was arising from the depths, and the woman in blue was very concerned. She didn't know what to do. What to expect. She closed her eyes and a magical coating went onto the individual threads in her loom. Each thread represented a life, a human life, and she was the Guardian, the one to watch over them all.

She looked outside her window, from a tower made of gold, silver, and rubies. The sky was a bloody red, and the wind was an ocean of screams. The woman with long, jet black hair shivered. Soon, it would be time. Soon, it would BE TIME.

ABOUT ALISON CLARKE

Alison Clarke is the Award Winning Canadian writer of The Sisterhood Stories, a collection of fantasy works that celebrate myths, legends and stories through the ages. She is an Afro-Canadian author who is passionate about increasing representation of strong, black female characters in a genre that has often woefully under, and mis-represented, Persons of Colour.

In 2016 she was awarded 'Writer of the Year Award' by Diversity Magazine Canada.

Alison loves meeting readers and spreading the word, she is an enthusiastic supporter of oral storytelling events and arts events that celebrate the diversity and power of all voices.

Alison is not only a novelist but a poet, painter, scholar, and adventurer.

This is the second book in her series.

OTHER WORKS

The Sisterhood.

Join us at www.thelittlebirdbookstore.com for more unique, quality reads of all genres and for all audiences.

Made in the USA
Columbia, SC
15 October 2017